WRECKED

ALSO BY E. R. FRANK

America

Friction

Life Is Funny

WRECKED

E. R. FRANK

Simon Pulse

NEW YORK   LONDON   TORONTO   SYDNEY

SIMON PULSE

An imprint of Simon & Schuster Children's Publishing Division

1230 Avenue of the Americas, New York, NY 10020

Copyright © 2005 by E. R. Frank

All rights reserved, including the right of reproduction in whole or in part in any form.

SIMON PULSE and colophon are registered trademarks of Simon & Schuster, Inc.

Also available in an Atheneum Books for Young Readers hardcover edition.

Designed by Kristin Smith

The text of this book was set in Aldine 401.

Manufactured in the United States of America

First Simon Pulse edition April 2007

2 4 6 8 10 9 7 5 3 1

The Library of Congress has cataloged the hardcover edition as follows:

Frank, E. R.

Wrecked / E. R. Frank.—1st ed.

p. cm.

"A Richard Jackson Book."

Summary: After a car accident seriously injures her best friend and kills her brother's girlfriend, sixteen-year-old Anna tries to cope with her guilt and grief, while learning some truths about her family and herself.

ISBN 0-689-87383-2 (hc.)

ISBN-13: 978-0-689-87383-6 (hc.)

[1. Traffic accidents—Fiction. 2. Death—Fiction. 3. Grief—fiction. 4. Guilt—Fiction. 5. Brothers and sisters—Fiction. 6. Self-acceptance—Fiction. 7. Family problems—Fiction.] I. Title.

PZ7.F84913Wav 2005

[Fic]—dc22 2004018448

ISBN-13: 978-0-689-87384-3 (pbk.)

ISBN-10: 0-689-87384-0 (pbk.)

For Jim

BEFORE

THE DAY I KILLED MY BROTHER'S GIRLFRIEND STARTED WITH ME handpicking leaves off our front lawn.

"Did you lose an earring, Anna?" Mrs. Caldwell called. She was wearing navy blue sweats with white racing stripes up the sides.

"Um," I called back. "Yeah." She stepped onto our brick pathway, probably to help me look.

"Oh," I said, loud, before Mrs. Caldwell could get too close. "Got it." I held my hand high in the air, as if I was showing her something I'd found. She nodded and then turned around right as my brother, Jack, backed the Honda out of our garage, music blasting.

"You want to help?" I called. I mean, he could have helped.

"Nope." He let the car roll slowly backward. "Sorry." He didn't sound sorry. But still. I guess I wouldn't have helped either. He cranked the music up even louder.

"What is that?" I shouted. He's always listening to bands nobody's heard of.

"Barking Duck!" Which is what it sounded like.

"Do you like it?" he asked, turning the volume down.

"Very funny," I said. "And don't forget, I have the Honda tonight."

"You won't need it if you don't finish the lawn."

And then he left me there, picking up crunchy brown leaves the size of hair clips. Picking them up, one by one, and dropping them into a plastic grocery store bag. Exactly the way my father had insisted. Not raking, because that might damage the grass. Not leaf blowing, because the noise was too loud and the gas smelled. Not watching some crew, because why should my father hire other people to do his lawn work when he had two perfectly able-bodied teenagers?

My mom poked her head out our front door, holding my cell. Damn. I thought I had it clipped to my back pocket. "It just rang." She had the top flipped up. "I think it was Ellen."

I blew out a big breath of air and straightened.

"Do you want company?" She has a bad back, so it went without saying that she wasn't going to help.

"No, I don't want company," I snapped. "I want not to do this."

"Is it such a big deal?" My mom handed me the cell.

"It's ridiculous, Mom." I put a lot of emphasis on the *dic* of *ridiculous*.

"Well," she said. Then she went back into the house.

I pick͟   ͦ more leaves and dropped them with the
others. ͙   ͟ something weird happened. I didn't plan it.
I hadn't   ͻeen thinking about it. But all of a sudden I
opened   ͟stic grocery bag, turned it upside down, and
dragged   ough the air. I watched the leaves scatter sideways ar   ͫn spiral downward toward the wispy blades
peeking   ͗om where my father had made Jack sprinkle
seed las   kend. How do they say it? *In one fell swoop.* Well,
in one   woop I dumped out all those leaves I'd been so
stupidl͟   ͥering up. Just dumped them right out.

I re͟   ͻer that moment as clear as the accident.
Someti   ͟learer. Who knows why.

WE'RE AT ELLEN'S. SHE'S FLATTENING HER BROWN HAIR, SLICKING it back into one long ponytail.

"It's too early to leave," she's saying. "Things won't get going until at least twelve."

"Well, it's twelve now," I tell her. "And we're still not ready."

"You want to call Lisa and them, and see where they are?"

I dial, and some guy answers. "What's up?" There's giggling in the background.

"Seth!" the giggler goes. I think it might be Lisa. "Give it back!"

"Is Lisa there?" I ask.

Ellen and I are sort of between groups right now. Last year we hung out a lot with this other Anna, and Katy and Slater and Kevin and Trace. But the other Anna switched schools, and Katy and Slater started wearing black lipstick and shaving their heads and telling us we were conformists, and Kevin and Trace started dating each other and never hanging out with anybody else, and things just sort of dissolved from there.

"Give it!" I hear Lisa shouting over her own giggles.

"What's going on?" Ellen asks.

"I think it's Seth. That guy who wears the sleeve," I say. A sleeve is this thing that looks sort of like a combination of a glove with no finger coverage and a sock that fits all the way up to your elbow. Other than the sleeve, Seth's pretty cute.

"Oh," Ellen goes. "Sleev-eth."

"Listen," I tell the phone. "Could you put Lisa on?" I try to sound sarcastic and bossy, but I'm not so good at that. Ellen is slightly better at it than I am. Neither of us is nearly as masterful as the Ashleys. Which is fine, because we have no desire to be complete bitches. Just to know how when necessary.

"Who's this?" Seth asks.

"Who is it?" I hear Lisa say.

"Give her the phone, man," some other guy complains.

"This is Anna," I say. "Ask Lisa if she's going to the party at Wayne's."

"Yeah." It's still Seth. "We're going. Is this Anna Lawson?"

I cover the phone with my hand. "Ellen," I whisper. "Sleev-eth knows who I am."

"Good," she goes.

"How do you know who I am?" I ask into the cell.

"It's me," Lisa says. I guess Sleev-eth gave hers back. "We're leaving in fifteen minutes."

"Us too," I say. "Ellen's taking forever to do her hair."

"I am not," Ellen goes. "Ask if they have beer." Ellen's developed

6

a taste for alcohol lately. I haven't. I don't like beer, for one thing. For another, I do like knowing what's going on.

"Do you guys have beer?" I ask.

"Yeah, plus Jack Daniel's."

"They've got Jack Daniel's," I tell Ellen.

"Where did they get that?"

"Anna?" It's Sleev-eth again.

"Seth!" I hear Lisa scream. Then the signal goes dead.

I flip down my phone. Ellen tugs at her ponytail and then turns from her mirror to look at me.

"You don't want to go, do you," she says.

"Yeah I do."

"You wanted to bitch some more about your father and then see *Rocky Horror.*"

"Maybe. But it's too late." *Rocky Horror* always starts at midnight.

"I kind of like parties now," Ellen tells me. Neither of us used to. Last year we would go to the mall instead. Or to Top Hats, our favorite diner. We thought parties were stupid up until about a month ago.

"I like parties too," I lie.

"No you don't. You always nurse a beer and stay in one place the whole time."

I don't know what to say to that. Ellen's been my best friend since we were nine. She knows me better than anybody. Really, anybody.

"You don't like me anymore," I sulk. "You're going to get in with the Ashleys and break them up and be one of their best friends and dump me." I'm only half kidding.

"Don't be stupid," she goes. "I just want to have some fun."

"Well, I do too," I say.

"Since when?"

"Since today."

"Oh, yeah?" she asks. "Do I have your dad to thank for that?"

"Whoever you want to thank," I tell her. "But I'm going to have fun flirting with Sleev-eth. And I'm going to have fun drinking."

She's always said I'm more of a stoner than a drinker, if I ever had the guts to do either. I've always said it's not about guts. It's just that I don't want to do drugs because if I got caught or something bad happened, my father would kill me. That's where Ellen usually rolls her eyes, and I wonder if she actually knows me better than I know me, and then I get nervous if I don't switch the subject in my head.

"Well, don't have too much fun," Ellen's warning me now, "because one of us has to be able to drive."

"Okay," I say. "Then, I'll just flirt."

"Good," Ellen goes. "Let's leaf now."

"Ha," I tell her.

Wayne's house is sort of like mine. Old and big with a huge front and back lawn. Which makes me think about my father and the fight we had before I left.

"You will not leave this house until that grass is taken care of," my dad said. He isn't used to me not doing what he asks. I'm not used to it either. But whatever it was that made me dump out those leaves earlier wouldn't let me give in.

"No," I argued. I was already late. I'd told Ellen I'd be there ten minutes ago. I was working hard to keep my head from going fuzzy, the way it gets when my father has me trapped somehow. Because even though I'm usually sure that it's something the matter with him that starts it all, I always end up feeling like there's something worse the matter with me for not seeing things his way.

So I tried to sound reasonable. My dad likes reasonable. "I'm sorry I didn't do it already," I said, as calm as I could. "But it's dark out now. Plus, it doesn't make sense to hand pick up leaves. I'll rake tomorrow, but tonight I'm going to Ellen's." Then I held my breath and started walking through the kitchen. Jack was at the table, waiting for his girlfriend to come over and typing some new movie review, probably, onto his Web site. Or maybe checking his UCLA admissions status.

"Stop," my father ordered. I didn't stop. "You stop right there." The fuzz went black while he moved in front of me to block the mudroom door. Jack didn't even look up. He can get so absorbed in whatever he's doing that he wouldn't notice if a hurricane hit.

"Dad!" I said.

I heard my mother's hard-soled shoes clack on the stairs. My father was standing so close I could feel the heat of him on me. "Give me the keys," he ordered.

"No. You're being totally unfair!" The black was getting worse, the way it does when he won't back off, which is all the time, and you can't do anything, you're just stuck, and everything turns into a massive knot of confusion. Jack glanced up at both of us right then, but only for a second.

"Harvey," my mother said, clacking into the kitchen. "What's going on?"

"She didn't pick up the leaves." The vein over his left eye was popped out. His face was shiny.

"I saw her pick up the leaves," my mother told him in that ultrapatient tone of voice she gets when he's like this. His jaw muscles started jumping.

"So did I." Jack snapped closed his laptop, scraped back his chair, and walked out.

I tried to clear the messiness in my head. It works better if you stay calm. Even though my father never does. His face was turning purple. I looked at my mom. "I told him already," I said evenly. "I'll rake tomorrow."

"Not rake!" my father exploded. He was frothing at the mouth. Seriously. Spit was gathering at the corners like he had rabies or something. "Not tomorrow. Pick. Up. Now!"

My mother was just standing there, lips in a tight, straight line. That *This is not right, but there's nothing I can do* look. I couldn't take it. I wasn't going to let him ruin my whole night. Make me get on my knees under the spotlights out front, as if I were some kind of psych patient, when he was the insane one.

I stepped around my father and through the mudroom, into the garage.

"If you leave this house, you will be extremely sorry!" he shouted right as I was yanking open the car door.

I jumped into the Honda. "If I come back to this house," I shouted back through the open window, "you will be extremely lucky!" And then I cried the whole way to Ellen's.

Wayne's got two sound systems going: one on the third floor and one on the first. Outside you can hear them both. House from the top. Disco from the bottom. They don't mix too well.

"See anybody we know?" I ask Ellen. We're trying to make our way inside. Ellen's always cold, so unless it's seriously summer, we never stay outdoors.

"No." She weaves through the crowd. Then when we walk in through the garage, she points. "There's Jason." I don't really know Jason. He's this guy in her history class Ellen has a crush on. He sees us and waves us over.

"Lisa and her friend were looking for you," he tells Ellen. "They went up to the third floor."

"Come with us," Ellen invites him. "This is Anna. Anna, this is Jason."

"Hi," we both say, and then we all start trooping upward.

On the stairs someone has taped signs that read, PLEASE DO NOT PARTY ON THE SECOND FLOOR. They're written in red marker on graph paper.

"There they are," Lisa says when she sees us. We're in a bedroom. Wayne's probably. It's got posters of bands and supermodels all over the place and beer-can pyramids everywhere. Lisa and Seth and a couple of other people are sitting on the bed. The house music is pounding. You can feel it buzz in your chest. *Thrum, thrum.* "You want some?" Seth offers us a bottle of Jack Daniel's with his right hand. With his left he's eating a peppermint patty.

"You guys know Jason?" Ellen asks, taking the whiskey. Everybody nods. My whole body keeps thrumming with the beat of the music. *Thrum, thrum.* "Where did you guys get it?"

"Bought it," Lisa goes. "Seth's got a fake ID." He does look sort of old. Not twenty-one, exactly. But with a fake ID I guess he can pass.

"You're Jack's little sister, right?" Seth asks me. This never used to happen.

"Where's your sleeve?" I ask him back.

"We convinced him to lose it," Lisa says.

"How do you know my brother?" I ask, even though I know how. But Seth's popped the rest of the peppermint patty into his mouth, so he can't answer.

"Ohhh," Jason goes instead. He takes a drink of Jack Daniel's. "Jack Lawson? You're Jack Lawson's little sister?" I still can't get used to having a brother who, practically overnight, has become a household name.

"Everybody knows your brother this year," Ellen tells me, like she's reading my mind. Which she kind of does a lot of the time.

"Cameron," I guess. Seth sighs. Jason and Lisa nod.

"Cameron Polk," they all say at once. *Thrum, thrum.*

Cameron Polk is Jack's girlfriend. His first girlfriend ever. They've been dating since the second week of school.

"Late," I said to Jack from his bedroom door, on the night I found out. He was sitting on that ergonomic chair in front of his laptop with the phone in his hand. He looked a little out of it. "Dinner," I said. "It's three minutes past." My parents had sent me to get him. My father wouldn't let me yell up the stairs. I had to walk up.

"Cameron Polk just agreed to go out with me Saturday night," Jack said.

"Really?"

He nodded. As far as I knew, he hadn't asked anyone out

since he was in the eighth grade, when Trisha Todd told him no because he was too short. He'd grown more than a foot since then, and mostly I thought of him as this annoying, gawky guy who lived in my house. Nobody ever messed with him exactly, and he and his best friend, Rob, weren't total outcasts or anything. But it wasn't like people loved Jack either. Then again, when I thought about it, looking at him with the phone in his hand, I realized that a lot of kids had started talking to him at the end of last year. Had he been getting cool, and I hadn't noticed it?

"*The* Cameron Polk?" I asked him.

She moved here the last month of school last year. She's one of these girls that you sort of can't believe. Nobody could stop looking at her. She's got smoky skin and shiny blond hair and this square jaw, with a little bit of slant to her eyes. She transferred into all the honors classes, and she seemed actually nice. No attitude. It took only three days before the Ashleys asked her to sit with them at lunch. She did a few times. But she sat with other people too. You can't get much classier than that.

"We're in French Five together," Jack told me.

I noticed that his shaggy hair and something about his jeans and T-shirt looked like this ad I'd seen in some magazine lately. Those ads where the guys never seem as if they care what they look like, but they look good anyway. Weird.

"Saturday's my night for the car," I reminded him.

"I know." He looked at the phone in his hand. "But."

"Anna!" we heard my dad yell up the stairs. "Jack!" He had that edge to his voice. It meant he'd be screaming for five minutes once we got down to the dinner table.

13

I stood there trying to think over the noise of my dad. I should let Jack have the car. It was a date. It was Cameron Polk. Obviously I should. It was just that I'd promised to drive to Jake Lowell's party so that Ellen could drink, and I didn't want Ellen to be mad. . . .

"Forget it," Jack said, and he had that expression I hate. That one where it's obvious he thinks I'm a disgusting human being. "Get out of my room."

"Anna!" my father shouted. "Jack!"

"Get. Out." When I didn't move, he stabbed a key on his keyboard, stood up, and brushed by me into the hallway.

"All right," I said to his back. "Fine. You can have the car on Saturday."

"Jack!"

"You know what?" my brother said, stopping at the top of the stairs. "Sometimes you are so small."

So now I get it. "Is that how you know who I am?" I ask Sleev-eth. He's holding out the whiskey, and I take it.

"Are you really going to drink tonight?" Ellen asks me.

I ignore her and keep talking to Seth. "Because you know who Jack is because everyone knows who Cameron is?" Then I take a huge, and I mean huge, swallow. And nearly choke to death. Jason kindly pounds me on the back for a while.

Ellen says, "Take a smaller swallow and go slower."

While I do, Seth goes, "No. I'm always seeing your hair in the hall." *Thrum, thrum.*

I have copper-colored corkscrew hair. No joke. Coils and coils of the stuff. It would be bad enough to have just the color.

And bad enough to have the corkscrews. Having both is the worst. Ellen and my mother say it's "adorable" and "striking." Right. Try *freakish.*

"I've been dying to pull it all year," Seth says. Then he reaches out, grabs a curl, stretches it down straight, lets it go, and watches it bounce right back.

"Supreme," he says.

"If we were in third grade," I inform him, "you'd so be in the corner right now."

"If we were in the third grade," Seth informs me, "I'd so be kicked out of school right now." He reaches out and pulls another curl.

"I hated that in the third grade," I warn him.

"She loves it now," Lisa says with a smirk. As if she even knows me.

I hold out the bottle to Ellen. She takes it and drinks.

"We're co-opting your liquor," I tell Sleev-eth. I'm having fun.

Here's when I first noticed Jack trying with me, after a lot of years of not. It was this past summer, the first Friday of our annual two-week beach vacation at Commons End. We'd just arrived at that year's rental house after a five-hour drive. Which should have been three hours, but the shortcut my father thought would shave off ten minutes ended up getting us lost. So whatever.

"Anna," Jack called up to me. I was on the elevated deck, hauling my suitcase and my mother's. It was dusk but still hot from the sun of the day. I could feel my skin prickle from sweat and aggravation.

"What?" I asked him.

"You want me to unpack so you can go check out the water?"

"Huh?"

It's always Jack and me who have to take everything out of the car and indoors. My father usually insists on packing the trunk before we leave, which involves a lot of impatience and yelling because he's sure that not everything will fit. Then, on the arrival end, he never helps unload. And with her bad back, my mom can't do much either.

"I'll unpack," Jack said. "You want to go see the ocean before it's dark, right?"

It was something we usually raced each other for. Who would get their half finished the quickest, jog the two blocks, scramble up the narrow dune path, and reach the peak first. Who would get to throw off shoes, slip-slide down, pad across the warm sand, and wade into the undertow, looking out onto the choppy green water, before the other one even showed up. It was usually too late to actually swim. But most years getting that first piece of the beach on the day we arrived was a part of starting things off.

"You mean, you'll unpack the whole car?" I asked Jack.

"Yeah." I watched his face, trying to figure out the trick.

"Okay," I said finally.

When I got back, we ate dinner, and after that Jack wandered through my door, listening to his iPod. My room had twin beds with ugly flowered curtains that matched the bedspreads, and a fake bamboo chair. I was on my cell phone, lying on the floor with my feet up on one bed. Jack did the same next to me. Not knowing what else to do, I said to Ellen, who was planning to come down three days later, "So, this is weird. Jack just came into my room and, like, made himself comfortable. He doesn't even have his laptop with him or anything."

He didn't so much as blink, and with his music on I couldn't even be sure he'd heard me. When I hung up with Ellen a few minutes later, Jack said, "Do you like Straw Man Proposal?"

I rolled my eyes. "You know I've never heard of them."

"Listen to this," he said instead of telling me what a moron I was. And he leaned over to plug his earphones into my ears.

I listened. It wasn't bad.

2

SOMEHOW ME AND ELLEN AND SETH AND LISA AND JASON AND these two other guys and this one other girl wearing a hot pink jean jacket end up in Wayne's basement playing pool. Which is fun, especially since I'm sort of good at it, and Sleev-eth and I are on the same team, and he's good too. Three swigs of the Jack got me way drunk for a few hours, but now I think I'm sobered up. For a while there I thought I was going to puke, but Ellen walked me twice around the entire house, even all around the second floor.

"Walking off too much alcohol doesn't exactly count as partying," she said when we passed some of those red-markered signs.

"Yeah, but we're not supposed to be here," I moaned. "The second floor! Wayne will be soooo mad."

"Wayne is soooo stoned right now he wouldn't be able to tell the second floor from the fifteenth," Ellen told me. "Now, keep walking."

"Do you think I'm going to pass out?" I was sort of hopeful. I'd never passed out before.

"Nah," she said. "If I thought you were that far gone, I'd throw you in the shower." That probably got me sober faster than anything.

"You're the best, El," I told her.

"Ugh," she said. "You are not a cute drunk."

But now I'm fine, and Ellen is having a hard time holding her pool cue. She had four beers on top of three shots of Jack Daniel's, all in the last hour and a half. And right as I'm realizing that I also realize our curfews are way over.

"Oh my God," I say, scratching my shot.

"What's wrong?" Sleev-eth asks. He's finishing another peppermint patty. I think I've seen him eat four tonight. And he's not even a little bit fat.

"Ellen, we have to go." I stand up and hand off my pool cue to Jason. "I'm in such deep shit."

"About time," Ellen says to Jason and the others. "She never does Anna-thing wrong." It's hard to believe she can do her word thing so drunk. Then again, *Anna-thing* is an old one.

"You have to go now?" Seth sounds bummed, which is nice.

"Just stay," Lisa goes. "You're already late anyway."

"You don't know my dad," I tell her.

"You're not driving," Jason warns Ellen.

"I am," I say, pulling the keys out of my back pocket. My key ring is a teeny, tiny glow-in-the-dark planet Earth. If you sit in the pitch black with it, it's got all the greens and blues and whites and the shapes of the continents and everything. Ellen gave it to me the day I got my learner's permit. "Now you've got the world at your fingertips," she'd said.

"Bye," I tell everybody. Seth pulls one of my curls.

"See ya," they say.

"Bye." Ellen flaps her hands at them and stumbles.

"Come on," I go, and I lead her from the pool table, up the stairs and out the front door, down the street, to the Honda.

"Eech," Ellen goes on Ocean Road.

"You want me to pull over and walk you around a little?"

"Eech," she says again. Then she leans over and against her seat belt to crank up the radio. It's that old U2 song. That ancient one: "Hoow loong to sing this soong? Hooow looong, hooooow loooong, hoow loong . . ." Ellen cranks it loud, and then she turns to me and she goes, "Do you think—"

And then there's this deafening smacking sound and the smell of new plastic, and Ellen in my lap, dripping with blood, and there's pieces of something falling and all this dust everywhere and chips flying up from the floor, and Ellen bloody with her head pressed hard against my collarbone, and the sharp brush of her ponytail sticking my right eye. "Hooow looong, hoow loong, hoow loong . . . ," and the sound of somebody screaming and screaming and screaming, and then somehow my door opens and I fall out with bloody Ellen half on top of me and her ponytail still sticking me in my eye, and I think, *How could she be in my lap and how could we fall out with our seat belts on?* And I keep hearing that screaming and screaming and screaming and screaming, and then I hear the screaming stop, and instantly I vomit all over myself and all over Ellen's head. "To sing this sooong?" And a man's voice says, "Three seven oh one," and there's a siren and somebody's holding a blanket, and another man's voice says, "Can you talk?" and I say, "My friend is bleeding," and then Ellen slides away, and her ponytail slides away with her, and the music stops, and then there's three policemen standing over me, and one of them wears Harry Potter glasses, and one of them is licking his lips, and the other one is saying something, only I can't make out the words, and I go, "I can't hear you," and I see the glow-in-the-dark earth dangling from somewhere really high up, and I'm looking at it and telling the cop, "I was going to do it tomorrow. I swear. I was going to do it tomorrow," and he stops talking to me, and he looks at the other two, and the Harry Potter one pulls off his glasses and turns away, and the one who was licking his lips turns with him, and I'm watching the earth swing gently back and forth, and that last cop leans down to me and tries again, and this time I hear him, and he's saying in this really friendly voice, "Okay. Okay. Okay. Okay."

3

I WANT TO VOMIT, AND MY RIGHT EYE THROBS. I GO TO TOUCH IT, when I hear someone say, "Don't do that." I open my eyes, except only the left one seems to be working. A nurse calls out to someone behind her, "She's waking up."

I feel panic spreading through my blood, like ink in water.

"Anna?" It's my mother.

"What are you wearing?" I go. Even with one eye I can see her long raincoat over pajamas.

"Anna," she says again. Blue-and-white-checked cotton. A raincoat over pajamas? Something is very wrong. I reach up again to my eye, but Mom grabs my hand.

"Don't," she says. "You have a shield on it. Leave it."

"Is Dad mad?" I say, and she starts to cry. Seeing that is so strange it makes me remember everything. Scattering the leaves in one fell swoop, and Ellen bloody in my lap. And screaming, stopped.

"Ellen." The panic is seeping everywhere. "Is Ellen okay?"

"She has a collapsed lung," my mom tells me. "And some broken bones." She blows her nose. The nurse fiddles with something above me, and I notice I've got a needle sticking in my arm. An IV.

"A collapsed lung?" I go. "That's bad, right?"

My mother nods.

"Is it days later?" I ask. I think it is. I think the accident must have happened at least a week ago.

"No, Anna," my mom says. She picks up my hand and squeezes it. "It's the same night. It's five thirty in the morning."

"What bones did Ellen break?" My eye is killing me. The throb fills up my entire head.

"Some ribs and her leg."

"Did I break anything?" I ask. Because it's hard to tell.

"No," my mom says. "You just injured your eye."

"My body hurts."

"Where?" Mom asks.

"Everywhere."

"We'll get the doctor. He'll want to talk to you."

"Where is Ellen?" My mom's chin starts to work a little again, and I feel the ink oozing into my chest.

"Intensive care," my mom finally says.

Maybe it's going to be Ellen who will wake up days later.

"Is she in a coma?" I don't know why I ask that exactly. Maybe because that's what usually happens on TV. My mother shakes her head and lets go of my hand to stroke my left arm. The one without the IV. Sometimes people don't wake up from comas. Sometimes people just stay vegetables. Ellen. A vegetable. I can hear her say it: *veg-Ellen-table.*

"Is she going to die?" I ask.

"No," my mother says. "She's not in a coma, and she's not going to die." Suddenly I'm really tired.

"She better not," I say. It's hard to get the words out. To speak.

"She won't," my mother says. It doesn't sound like she's lying, but a collapsed lung is bad. I'm pretty sure that's bad. And there's something else going on, something to do with the panic. I can't relax.

She's still stroking my left arm.

"Mom," I say, *why are you petting me?* But I don't have enough energy. "Mom" is all I say.

Later I still feel sore all over, and my eye throbs along with my whole skull. There's a sideways sliding tray set up in front of me. Scrambled eggs, toast, a small cup of purple jelly, and orange juice are sitting on it. I have to pee. Badly. I shove the tray out of my way and realize there's no needle in my arm anymore.

"Hello?" I go. The door to my little room is open, and with my left eye I can see nurses and people walking back and forth. "Hello?"

My mother rushes in. Now she's wearing regular clothes. Her light leather jacket, jeans, and clogs.

"Anna?" she says.

"I have to go to the bathroom."

She helps me. It's strange to stand up. It makes my entire

head pulse, for one thing, and my legs feel wobbly and splayed, like a newborn foal's. I have to lean on my mother to walk the five steps to the toilet. Which is strange too.

There's a mirror above the bathroom sink. My mom hustles me through washing my hands, but I see myself long enough to get nauseous again. My hair is a mass of orange snakes. The thing on my eye looks like a miniature spaghetti strainer. Silver-colored metal, pricked with little holes. Around the sticky, white-tab edges of it my skin is swollen and blue. I try not to imagine what's underneath.

"Is it Sunday?" I ask after I'm safe back in bed. My mother sits in a chair next to me. For some reason I still feel like I must have blacked out, and for much longer than she's saying.

"Yes."

"Last night was the accident?" I ask, just to be sure. She nods. "Where's Dad and Jack?"

My mother looks awful. Huge gray circles under her eyes, white lips, stringy hair. Like she hasn't slept all night. Which, now that I think about it, she probably hasn't. "Mom?" I say again. "Where are they?"

"Anna," she says, taking my hand again.

"What?" I won't let her hold it. Something's not right. That ink seeps through me. I can't relax. "Dad's really, really mad, right?" I say, but some part of me knows that's not it.

"Do you remember what happened last night?" she asks.

"Yes," I say. "What does that have to do with Dad not being here?" The aching in my eye and head drops straight to my throat. My body starts to tremble. My whole body. It just starts to shake.

"Do you realize that there was another car involved?" my mother goes.

There was screaming. Screaming and screaming and screaming. It wasn't Ellen, and it wasn't me. *"Hoooow looong, hooow loooong . . ."* And then the screaming stopped. It stopped because the life stopped. Somehow I knew it then. I know it now. I don't need anybody to tell me. I heard the life stop.

I feel the ache come out of both my eyes in tears, and I try not to cry, but it's hard not to cry, and it makes me shake more. My mom sees it. The shaking. My teeth are chattering. She climbs onto the bed. She spoons behind and wraps her arms around me tightly to try to keep me still. But I can't stop shaking.

"Anna, listen to me," she says. Her breath is warm on my neck and in my ear. "The driver of the other car died."

"I know," I try to tell her, but my jaw and mouth are chattering so much, I can't make the words.

"Anna," my mother says. She pulls her arms even tighter, and I'm glad because I think I might shake myself right off the bed onto the floor if she weren't here, holding me together. "It was Cameron Polk," she says. *Cameron Polk.* "Do you understand?" *Cameron Polk. Cameron Polk.* I make myself understand.

"Yes," I say, shaking.

"Do you understand?" she says again.

"Yes," I say.

4

THE NURSE IS EXPLAINING ABOUT MY EYE. ONE DROP A DAY TO help the pain, and another drop of something else to keep my pupil dilated so that there won't be rebleeding. Somehow I register the word *rebleeding,* and I wonder, vaguely, what that means. The nurse might be trying to tell me what it means, but I can't really understand what she's saying. I see her mouth moving, and I see my mother's listening face, and I even hear words, but it's like I'm underwater on Mars. Everything is blurry and foreign and floating.

Things get slightly more clear and still and in focus after my mother leaves me to call my dad and check on what's happening with him and Jack. I wobble out into the hallway and ask another nurse where intensive care is, and she tells me, even though I think she won't. While she's saying I should go back to my room and wait for my mom to come get me, I get myself into the elevator and hold on to the metal bar on the way up to the fifth floor. Right as the elevator door opens I see the Gersons rushing down the hall in the opposite direction from me, so I make my way to the end of the hall where they were coming from, and I check a few doors, and the third door is where I find Ellen.

Even with half vision, from ten feet away, feeling like I'm still underwater, I can see she's messed up. I ache all over, and I'm stiff as anything, and my whole head is pounding, with the center of the pound right in the middle of my right eye, even with the drops for pain, so it takes a while to get near Ellen's bed.

Besides two IVs, one in each arm, there's a tube that goes from under the covers to a bag with what I'm sure is pee in it. She has a bandage on her left cheek, a big blue tube in her mouth that looks like a sicko accordion straw designed to choke you to death, and another tube that's attached to her somewhere, only I can't tell where because it disappears under the hospital blanket and sheets. She's asleep, I guess, only I'm worried she's in a coma. How do you know the difference, anyway?

"You look like shit," I tell her. She turns her head the littlest bit. "I threw up on you." She opens her eyes, and for a second I think she sees me, but then she closes them again. I hear this slow whooshing sound, but I can't tell which machine it's coming from.

"Hey," a male nurse says, walking in. "You're not supposed to be here."

Ellen is really still now. The whooshing keeps going, though.

"You need to leave," this nurse says. He's got hair the same color as mine. "What floor did you come from?"

"I killed Cameron Polk," I whisper to Ellen.

Nothing.

I'm sitting in a wheelchair, waiting for my parents to come get me. The hospital doesn't let you walk out. They make you wheel out. I'm thinking about how stupid that is and trying to block the screaming, stopped, out of my head, when my dad walks in.

"Hi," I say.

My heel starts uncontrollably tapping the footrest of the wheelchair.

"Anna," my dad says, and the next thing I know, he's kneeling and hugging me hard, careful not to touch my right eye.

"Is the Honda totaled?" I ask.

"I don't care about the car," he answers, which is a complete lie and really nice of him to say. Especially because he hugs me tighter when he says it, even though it's hard to hug when one person's in a wheelchair and when you can see that her heel is clattering like a mini jackhammer.

Driving home, it's mostly my father who talks. My mom lets me sit up front in the Audi and stays quiet.

"Jack is . . ." My dad stops and clears his throat. "Jack's not doing well," he tells me. I try to picture my brother. It's hard, for some reason. "He's pretty broken up." My mother's hand finds my shoulder and rests there. I look out the window and wonder how long she's going to keep it there, warm and light, and notice how the shield over my eye itches me around the edges.

"Was it my fault?" I ask. My father doesn't answer right away.

He turns left on Pelham, taking the long way home. "Was it my fault?" I ask again. "The accident?"

"She was on your side of the street," my father says. She was? "Were you speeding?"

I shake my head. He makes a left onto Ladyshire. And then I figure out what he's doing. He's avoiding Ocean Road. He's avoiding where it happened.

"Were you drunk?"

"I don't think so," I say.

"What do you mean, you don't think so?"

I feel black fuzz start to mix with the ache behind my eye, and I try to stay clear.

"I had two shots of Jack Daniel's a long time before I drove," I say, waiting for the yelling. "Two or three hours before."

"Your blood-alcohol level was under the legal limit." My father's not raising his voice. He doesn't mention anything about the fact that I shouldn't have been drinking at all. "Were you speeding?" he asks again.

"I don't think so," I say. "I was about to pull over for Ellen. We thought she might be sick."

"Her blood-alcohol level was three times the legal limit," my father informs me.

I'm not surprised. Everybody's quiet for a while. And I still need to know for sure.

"So." I'm kind of shaking again. My fingers are quivering. "Was it my fault?"

"No." My mother's hand tightens on my shoulder before my dad can answer. "She was in your lane."

When we come around the curve in our street, so that I can see my house, there's a figure kneeling on the grass. As we get closer and pull into the driveway I can see that it's Jack.

"What's he doing?" my mother asks. I look out the window with my one good eye, and Jack glances up with his two.

He's picking leaves off the lawn.

5

WHEN WE WERE LITTLE, WE GOT ALONG REALLY WELL. ESPECIALLY at the beach. Every day of our two-week summer vacation at Commons End we would play in the surf, facing the choppy green expanse for hours. Our parents would be lying on the shoreline, under the shade of two umbrellas, covered with sun-block, broad-brimmed hats, and wraparound sunglasses. They'd be reading in low-slung chairs, legs outstretched, bottoms of their feet encrusted with wet sand.

My brother and I would locate ourselves exactly in the path of the breakers, giddy with the challenge of negotiating those endless waves. We'd dive into a curl and pop up and out the other side, braced for the next. We'd shoot our bodies vertically over a crest, letting the edge of it slap hard at our necks. Lie on our backs, feet forward, bobbing toward the sky with a slow-moving swell. Duck low and deep when our timing was off on a rough rogue, holding our breath beneath the frenzy, desperately waiting for it to pass over. Bodysurf until our bellies scraped sand, then fight the tide to get back in. Wipe out every now and then, the ocean flinging us underwater into a spinning knot of suffocating, airless panic. Bump and slip and hurl ourselves into each other's bony arms and legs. And then, dozens and dozens of waves later, with blocked ears, salty, snotty upper lips, and burning eyes, Jack would look at me and say, "I'm going to stop the ocean."

He'd face the surf, plant his feet wide, all lean limbs and spiky hair and shiny skin. "Watch." He'd raise his arms, palms flat forward, a wave bearing down on us. "Stop!" he'd yell in his deepest voice. "I command you to stop!"

And for a second I'd think he could do it. I'd think the wave would freeze in its curl, cartoonlike in its obedience to my brother's power. But then it would be on us, tumbling our bodies under its smack, daring us to find our legs again.

"Stop!" he'd order the second one, arms out, like a traffic cop. "Stop! You will stop now!" But that one wouldn't stop either, and then, hurrying before the next hit, he'd pull at my shoulder, lining me up right next to him. "Anna," he'd say. "You've got to help." So I'd plant my feet wide, just like his, and throw out my palms, and I'd shout at the next wave, "Stop! Stop!"

And the two of us, blue-lipped and drenched, worn out and determined, would yell over and over and over, wave after wave after wave, "Stop! We command you to stop!"

6

THEY LET ME SLEEP LATE ON MONDAY. I SLEEP HARDER AND
deeper than usual. When I wake up, I'm so groggy it takes a
while for me to figure out that the heaviness in my blood and
the dread in my chest are because two nights ago I killed somebody. *Cameron Polk is dead.* And Ellen. Jack.

My eye is killing me. I sit up in bed, peel off the spaghetti
strainer, and reach for the eyedrops. It's hard. I miss a few times
with each bottle, and the liquid drips coldly down my cheek.

Things are clanging downstairs. Silverware drawer opening
and closing, dishes dropped into the sink. I press the shield back
into place, drag myself out of bed, and pull on jeans and a zip-up
sweatshirt.

My parents are in the kitchen drinking coffee and wiping
instant-oatmeal dust off the table.

"Don't you have classes?" I ask my mother. I rub my left eye. It has tons of crust in the corners. Gross.

She reaches to hug me. "Never on Mondays." She holds on for a long time, careful of my right eye. It's strange but good, like when she held me in the hospital bed. It's not that we don't get along, so much as we're not that close, I guess. The truth is, before yesterday I don't remember the last time we touched. "Just office hours," she's saying now, sipping at her mug. "Which I've cancelled."

She teaches Web design and computer skills at the community college. She always gets the highest marks on her student evaluation forms at the end of each semester. She has Jack or me look at them and give her the results because she says it's only a matter of time before her luck changes and they all start to hate her.

I wander over to the kitchen table, near my father. "I thought Russell was incompetent."

My dad works in finance. He invests other people's money, and he has this male secretary who he doesn't much like and who he thinks is going to accidentally bankrupt the clients and ruin us all forever.

"Russell is incompetent," my father says. "Which is why I'm going to work." He checks his watch. "In about five minutes. I just wanted to see you first."

"Here I am," I say. And then I want to cry, but my father doesn't like crying, so I look away. Still sitting, he pulls me in by the waist and doesn't say anything, which makes not crying harder.

"Why don't you just fire Russell?" I ask into the air over his head. It's an old question. It feels good to ask it, like everything's normal, like today's just another day. My father releases me.

"Because everybody's incompetent," he says. "And I'd rather deal with familiar idiocy than with unfamiliar idiocy." It's what he always answers, and it helps me pretend that my hands aren't trembling and that I'm not sore all over and that I didn't kill anyone.

"How does your eye feel?" my mother asks. Which begins to ruin my pretending.

"Like it has a toothache," I tell her.

"We leave for the ophthalmologist in half an hour."

"Okay," I say.

"Then we'll see if you can visit Ellen." Now my legs are trembling a little too. I sit down and cross my legs and arms, try to hold everything still.

"Can I go wake up Jack?" I ask.

"No," they both say, right at the same time.

Dr. Pluto is all business.

"Hyphema," he tells me and my mom. He looks more like a football player than an ophthalmologist. His whole head is shaved, and he's huge. When he puts my face in this vise, his hand palms my head the way I'd palm a tennis ball.

"Are you still here?" I ask the room. Because I can't turn my head now.

"Behind you," my mom says from behind me and to the left. I didn't care if she came in or not. She wanted to, though.

First Dr. Pluto uses this machine to shine a vertical yellow light right at my eye.

"This is called a slit lamp," he tells me, even though I didn't ask. When he's done with that, he puts a drop in my eye, tells me the next procedure won't hurt, and fiddles with the vise a little.

"Does that feel okay?" he asks.

"I guess," I say. I mean, my head is in a vise.

Now it's a different machine. It moves closer and closer and closer, until it touches my eyeball really fast and there's this beautiful bright blue light everywhere, and then it's done.

"I'll need to see her every day to monitor the pressure and to make certain there's no rebleeding," Dr. Pluto tells my mother while she helps me get the strainer back on. "A hyphema is really just blood in the anterior chamber. It's a tear in the eye, probably from the air bag."

My mom asks him something, but I stop paying attention.

The air bag. The smell of new plastic. *"Hooow looong, hoow loong, hoow loong . . ."* Screaming, stopped.

Ellen's mom owns a women's clothing store called Cinnamon Toast. According to the tags of speckled brown paper on each item, Cinnamon Toast specializes in flowing styles and natural fibers. Usually Mrs. Gerson is wearing something in flowing style and natural fiber, and today is the same as always. Muted green slacks and a pale lavender blouse. She reaches for my face as soon as I walk into the fifth-floor waiting room. She cups my cheeks in her palms.

"That thing is awful," she tells me, meaning the shield, and she pulls me into lavender. "I'm so glad you're all right." She smells like Ellen's house: lemons and perfume. It's nice but embarrassing to be in her arms, so I ease away after a second.

"Are you all right?" Ellen's father asks, holding me, straight armed, by the shoulders and staring at my face. Aching in my eye. Aching in my throat.

"Yeah," I tell him. His eyes are swollen and bloodshot. "How's Ellen?"

"Well," Mrs. Gerson answers in this bright, fake voice. "She's got a tube in her mouth to help her breathe, a tube in her chest to reinflate her lung, an IV for antibiotics, an IV for pain, a catheter to help her pass water, a cast on her leg, and nothing for her ribs. They'll heal on their own."

"A collapsed lung is bad, right?" I say. Mrs. Gerson's attitude is confusing me. It doesn't match Mr. Gerson's face.

"She's going to be fine, Anna," Mrs. Gerson tells me. I see a nurse behind that long counter glance up and try to make eye contact with her, and I see her refuse to make eye contact back. That starts me shaking so hard both of the Gersons notice. Ellen's mom takes my hands and rubs them.

"She's going to be fine," she says again, loud.

"I'm really sorry." My teeth are chattering again. My eye radiates ache through my head. "I'm really, really sorry."

"It's not your fault," Mr. Gerson says. "They say there was a tree branch. Cameron must have swerved to avoid it."

A tree branch. I hadn't heard that yet. But if Cameron swerved to avoid a tree branch, couldn't I have swerved to avoid Cameron? I start to think about the alcohol and how drunk I was at first, and then how drunk Ellen was.

"Ellen doesn't have a drinking problem or anything," I tell them. "I mean, sometimes this year she would get pretty drunk at a party, but only twice." Oh my God. She's going to kill me for telling them this.

"Okay," her father says to me. His red eyes start welling up.

"We were always careful, though," I go on. I can't seem to

help myself. "We always were with each other, and we never drank with anybody we didn't know." Well. Almost never.

"Okay," Mr. Gerson says again. His eyes are all wet, but he doesn't cry.

He works for the same bank as my dad, only in some other area. Something higher up, I think. I don't know. They don't ever see each other at work. They have totally different responsibilities. And even though Mr. Gerson's got some big job and isn't a teller, I suddenly imagine how calm he'd be during a robbery. Some guy with a stocking over his head would be pointing the gun right at Mr. Gerson, and Mr. Gerson would just face him squarely, all steady.

"And she doesn't do drugs or anything, and it's not like she needs to drink when we go out. She doesn't do it at every party." Which, now that I hear myself saying it, might be sort of a lie.

"Okay," Mr. Gerson says a third time.

"Don't be mad at her," I tell them. When I say that, Mrs. Gerson starts to nod, but then her face collapses like Ellen's lung, and she's crying, and seeing Mrs. Gerson afraid is almost as shocking as Cameron Polk being dead.

"It's okay," Mr. Gerson tells her. He turns from me to face her. "It's okay."

He sounds like that policeman from the accident: *"Okay. Okay. Okay. Okay."* But it's not okay. Nothing is okay.

The Gersons let me see her for ten minutes. They leave the room for five.

"I called you," I tell Ellen. That whooshing sound would put me to sleep if it weren't paired with all those tubes and things, snaking right into her body or disappearing under the blanket. Today her left leg is over the covers. There's a bright white cast from just above her knee all the way to her toes.

"I left a message. Actually, I left eight. Did you get them?" I know she didn't because cell phones aren't allowed in hospitals. There's no phone in here. She can't talk anyway, with that tube in her mouth.

Her hair is dirty. It looks like somebody brushed it, but it really needs a shampoo.

"Pretty soon it's not going to be cell phones anymore," I say. She makes a sound, and I lean forward to listen better, but then she stops. I notice this other machine. A squarish clear plastic box with water in it. The water is making all these bubbles. I can't figure out what it's for.

"It's going to be these little chips that get implanted behind our ears. I read about it just now, while I was waiting to have my eye checked out. They didn't have any *People* magazines, so I had to read *Scientific American* instead. Actually, I didn't really read it. Mostly just the headline. Things are blurry up close with my right eye. But I'm allowed to use my left one. And TV is okay."

Ellen opens her eyes, and I move to where it seems like they're focusing, but by the time I adjust my position, they're closed again.

"No school for a week," I say. "I'm supposed to stay really still, and I have to wear this shield thing when I'm asleep and in a car." Now she moans. Definitely a moan. She moves her head a little. "El?" I go. She's still again. "I'm supposed to try not to sneeze," I say. "If I sneeze, it might tear inside my eye again, and then everything gets worse. Only, once you have to sneeze, it's impossible to stop yourself, you know?" She opens her eyes and looks straight at me. "El?" She stays looking at me. "Hi, Ellen," I tell her. I move closer. She keeps her eyes open for a second longer, and then she's gone again.

"I was thinking I should send Cameron's parents a letter or something," I say, listening to the whooshing and watching the bubbles in that plastic box. "That's what you think I should do, right?" I wait, and I hear the screaming, stopped, and try to shake it out of my mind. "My father is being slightly less of an asshole." I walk nearer to her bed. I touch her cast, by the ankle. It's hard and cold. "I'm going to write something on this," I tell her. I look around for a pen. There's one attached to a clipboard hanging from a peg on the door. I slip it off and think about what to write. I think and think and think, and I'm still thinking when the Gersons walk back in.

"I can't think of anything to write," I tell them when they see me at the edge of the bed with the ballpoint in my hand.

"How could you?" Mrs. Gerson says as if it's an argument and she's taking my side. She hands me a cup of coffee. I don't really drink coffee, but I like the heat in my palms. "For God's sake."

My mom and I get lunch out after the hospital, and she keeps touching my hand or my arm or some part of me, which is still so different from our usual, and we don't say a whole lot, which is the same as our usual, and she drives really, really slowly on the way home.

We don't get back until about three. Jack is in the family room, watching TV. Not watching a movie on DVD. Watching an actual television show. I walk in, my chest hot and pounding, and then I notice Rob is here.

"Hi," I say.

Rob nods. He's not a big talker.

"Thanks for coming over, Robert," my mother says, stopping in the family-room doorway. She stares at Jack, slides her palm along my arm, and then walks away.

"Why are you guys watching TV?" I ask. I can see the TV fine with my left eye. The throbbing is still pretty bad, though. It passes through my head like a steady wave.

Rob shrugs.

"You hate TV," I tell Jack. He picks up the remote and aims it at the screen. The TV goes black. Now my brother looks at me. I want to say things, but it's hard with Rob here. He's staring at my eye. He points to it and tilts his head.

"It's called a shield," I say.

"Why are your teeth chattering?" Rob asks next. His voice is really deep. I always forget how deep it is.

"They're not chattering," I lie, and then I clamp my jaw tight to stop them from doing it.

Jack's still looking at me. I guess I'm going to have to ignore Rob.

"Jack," I go. "I . . ."

He just looks.

"I didn't have time. I mean . . . I didn't even see her when . . ." Rob's face is turning red. Jack's face stays exactly the same. Why doesn't Rob just leave?

"Jack," I try again. But the words won't come.

Jack looks back at the still TV. "I'm glad you're okay," he says. His voice is as blank as the screen.

•   •   •

Cameron was good for us. I didn't get it then, but even from the first time I really met her, she helped Jack and me. It was just some school-day afternoon, right after they started going out. It wasn't any big deal.

"Oh my God," I yelled, throwing my hands over my ears. The kitchen looked like a war zone. "What happened?"

Pots and pans and flour and chocolate splotches and bunched-up dishrags and eggshell slime all over the place. Plus the smell of something burned, and what looked like soil sprinkled all over the kitchen floor, and some horrendous, unbelievably earsplitting music.

"Hi!" Cameron called to me. She was on her knees trying to sweep up the soil with the edges of her hands. "I'm Cameron!" As if I didn't know. "You must be Anna!"

Jack clomped in from the family-room side of the kitchen, hauling the vacuum cleaner. He was moving his mouth along with what I guessed were supposed to be lyrics. He stopped clomping and lip-synching the second he saw me. Then he was saying something, but I couldn't hear a word.

"What?"

He tried it again.

"What!"

Jack dropped the vacuum cleaner and hit the stop button on the CD player. I lowered my hands from my ears, and Cameron stood up.

"What happened?" I asked again in a normal voice.

"We're making a chocolate cake," Cameron said. Then she laughed. Not giggled. Laughed. One of those big, joyful, from-your-gut kinds of laughs. It was totally contagious. Well, it would have been with anybody other than Jack and me. He stood there looking bummed. I stood there feeling awkward. Cameron stopped laughing.

"Since when do you bake?" I asked Jack.

"Since today," he told me. "Weren't you going to the mall with Ellen?"

"We went," I told him.

"That's going to be much better," Cameron said about the vacuum cleaner.

"Did you drop a plant?" I asked them.

"We dropped the cake," Jack said.

"That's sweet," Cameron said. "Your brother is so sweet. *I* dropped the cake."

"Was it burned?" I asked. "It smells like something got burned."

"The first one burned," Cameron said. Then she started laughing again. "We kind of forgot about it, if you know what I mean."

Jack turned red. I think I did too.

"So. Good-bye," he said to me. He flicked the CD player back on. I clamped my hands over my ears again, and right away Cameron leaned over and turned it off.

"What's that about?" she asked Jack.

"What?"

"Can't your sister hang out with us?"

Jack and I both looked at her like she had four eyes and antennae.

"Now?" Jack asked.

"Um. Yeah," Cameron said. I didn't know what to do. On

the one hand, I really wanted to hang out with Cameron. On the other hand, that meant hanging out with Jack.

"We don't really hang out," I said finally. "Not since we were little kids." She curled a strand of shiny blond hair behind her left ear and then kept her fingers on her earlobe.

"Seriously?" she asked. It was embarrassing. All of a sudden I felt like there was something really wrong with us. Maybe Jack felt that way too, because he started humming. Just like my father does when he's tense. I guess Cameron heard a tune somewhere in there.

"Bid List?" Cameron asked him.

"Yeah," he said, smiling. It was this smile I sort of knew but sort of didn't. It reminded me of when he was a lot younger. "You know Bid List too?"

"I'm telling you," Cameron said. She was finished fiddling with her ear. "You better get into UCLA. Everybody in California likes the music you like."

"Nobody here has ever heard of it," I told her.

"That's what Jack says."

"Yeah, well. He's right." He looked at me, and I looked at him. Cameron looked at both of us and went to work on her earlobe again. Her left one.

"You're probably not as different from each other as you think you are," she told us.

"We're pretty different," Jack said. What was that supposed to mean?

"I'm not sweet," I told Cameron. "According to Jack, I'm small."

"Sometimes," he added.

She turned her back on us to start washing a cake pan at the sink.

"You guys even look alike," she said. "Except for the hair." We don't look anything alike. He's all dark skin and eyes and everything, and I'm orange and pale and blue.

"She's crazy," I told Jack.

"Hey," he said. But he was joking. "Don't call my girlfriend crazy."

She splashed water at him from the sink. Some of it splattered me. "Your girlfriend?" she said. "I have a name, you know."

"Yeah," I said to Jack. "She's got a name."

"You've got to vacuum, for that," Cameron told him. "I'll clear off the counters and start a new cake." She laughed again. "Third time's a charm. Anna, you wash."

So I swapped places with Cameron, and she let Jack put the music back on, only not so loud, and we all sort of did our thing in silence. When Cameron poured fresh batter into the pan I'd just cleaned, she said, "So, what's the deal?" She dipped a pink, pretty finger into the pan and then reached over to feed Jack, who had just stepped on the vacuum to turn it off. Oh my God. I looked out the window. I was not about to watch my brother lick cake batter off his girlfriend's finger. Off Cameron Polk's finger. "Do you guys hate each other or something?" she asked.

I waited awhile and then risked a glance at them. It seemed safe again. Jack was sitting on one of the counter stools, and Cameron was using the back of a spatula to spread batter evenly in the pan.

"Of course we don't hate each other," I said.

"You don't?" Jack asked.

"Do you?" I asked him back.

"Are you two kidding me?" Cameron said.

"No," we both said at the same time.

"It's Ellen. Leave a message. If this is Anna, try back in five minutes."

It's totally good to hear her voice, even though it's not live. I'm lying in my bed with my legs drawn up and one ankle resting across the other knee. It's late, and all my shades are down, and the only light in the room is the quiet blue from my cell phone. Before I would have my glow-in-the-dark key chain hanging off my big toe, and I'd be gazing at the earth. But that was before. It's lost now.

"Hi, Ellen. It's Tuesday. Everybody's totally psyched. They took that breathing tube out, which is a good thing. In a couple more days, after they're sure your lung isn't collapsed anymore, they'll take out the chest tube. I haven't been back to school yet. I'm bored out of my mind. Plus, I look like a cyborg with this shield thing I have to wear over my eye. Jack is freaked out. My father is being sort of nice and sort of not. After we went upstairs at Wayne's, I got really drunk and then you got really drunk and we were playing pool and then we were late, and I drove us home, and they say she swerved to avoid a tree branch, and it happened really fast, and I think you passed out right away. Your parents don't seem mad about the drinking. I told them not to be. You know it was Cameron, right? If they haven't told you, or if you think you dreamed it or something, it was Cameron in the other car. She died, Ellen. Just so you know. Call me as soon as you get this."

7

"YOUR BROTHER WAS REALLY GOOD," LISA GOES AFTER SHE HUGS
me, carefully, at my locker. The smell of shoes and hand lotion
and the sound of locker doors slamming make me feel a little
more normal than I've felt in a while. Maybe I'm not even
shaking all that much.

"Thanks," I say. Even though I was still just getting to know
her as of the night of the party, I'm really glad to see her now.

Dr. Pluto checks me every day with the tonometer—the
machine with the beautiful blue light. Last Friday he said
everything looked good enough that I could go back to school.
I have to wear the shield, though, and I have his note ordering
teachers to let me leave classes early so I can walk in quiet halls
and not get my eye whacked again by some joker tossing
around his backpack or a Frisbee or whatever. I decide I'll use

the note just sometimes. When I'm in a boring class. Like history, for example.

Jack started back last Thursday. Friday there was an assembly in honor of Cameron. Her funeral will be in California, where she used to live and where her parents have already returned. People are saying they couldn't stand to stay where she was killed. *Killed.*

Jack spoke at the assembly Friday. I only know that because my mother told me. Jack isn't not speaking to me exactly. But when he does, it's only for polite reasons. "Excuse me," he said yesterday as we brushed by each other going in and out of the first-floor bathroom. "Excuse me"? We'd never said "Excuse me" to each other in our entire lives.

"That memorial link to Rosebud Is a Sled is an amazing idea," Lisa tells me. Link? I don't know what she's talking about. I do know that Rosebud Is a Sled is Jack's movie review Web site. He designed it last year, and once I heard him tell Rob he'd gotten more than three thousand hits. I guess that means people actually use it. "Can he really get it ready that fast?" Lisa's asking me. "He said by next week."

"Yeah." I'm wondering how long I can get away with one-word responses before Lisa figures out that I don't know what the hell she's talking about.

"I'm not sure if I should post anything," Lisa's going. "I was thinking about it, except I didn't really know her. Then again, maybe I should just do a sentence or something so they get the five dollars." Five dollars? "Is Jack going to pick the charity the money goes to, or are Cameron's parents going to do that?"

"I don't know," I say. How could he have done that

already? How could he have thought of it and started it? "I think they're still figuring it out." How could the brother I saw less than a week ago on our front lawn–turned–psych ward have already spoken to the entire school and planned an entire link? An entire memorial Web site? I need to write a letter. I need to write Cameron's family a letter. Screaming, stopped. My eyes throb. Both of them.

"Are they letting people visit Ellen?" Lisa's asking me. Jason yanks at his lock across the hall, making sure it's locked, and then heads our way.

"Just family. She can talk now, but she's on serious drugs." Her parents said I could see her the day before yesterday, but when I got to the hospital, the doctor was there and he vetoed me for some reason.

It was weird to see the Gersons in the hospital but not to see Ellen. What made it weirder was the way the waiting room was decorated. It was strung with orange and black streamers and cardboard cutouts of black cats and broom-riding witches and a white ghost with big, friendly dimples. Halloween. I'd forgotten it was almost Halloween. I must have looked right at home with my robot eye.

"Hey," Jason goes, and he hugs me too. He has strong arms, and he holds on for more than a second. It feels good. "How are you?"

"Alive," I start to say, but, mortified, I stop myself and mumble some nonword instead.

"Does your eye hurt?" Jason asks, looking at my shield.

"No." I'm deciding right here and now that I won't complain again, ever, about anything that hurts me. That just seems like the right thing to do. If Cameron can't complain, why should I get to?

Everybody's quiet, and I don't like it. So I think of something to say. "Did you understand the math homework?" I ask Jason. He has precal fourth, and I have it fifth, but it's the same teacher. At our school if you miss a day, it's murder. I don't know how Ellen's going to catch up. I don't know how I am either. It's hard to read with just one eye.

"Not remotely," Jason says.

"Seth has been really worried," Lisa tells me.

Katy and Slater slide through the crowd of kids and walk over. Katy hugs me as if we've never stopped being friends. Is everybody going to hug me today?

"It's really good to see you," she goes. We nod in the halls this year, but we haven't really spoken at all.

"Thanks," I say. Her fingernails are polished black to match her lipstick, and she has a ring through her eyebrow. I'm nervous Lisa and Jason will think she and Slater are losers, which might make them think I'm a loser.

"That thing on your eye is excellent," Katy tells me.

"Tell Ellen we say hi," Slater adds. He's completely bald except for an orange tuft at the top center.

"Okay." I sort of just want them to go away, they're so weird. "I definitely will." They leave.

Lisa looks at me.

"Ellen and I were friends with them for a long time," I explain. "Whatever." And then I feel bad because I think Ellen will be happy they stopped me the way they did, and I'm not happy about it and I know that's sort of mean, but I can't help it.

"You know where that guy is going to be ten years from now?" Jason says. He means Slater.

"Who cares," Lisa goes.

"In a manly office, in a manly business suit, with a manly haircut, and a thing for men."

"Slater?" I go. "You think he's gay?"

"I do," Jason says. I guess he should know, since he's gay himself. According to Ellen, anyway.

"Do you think he's cute?" It didn't occur to me that anybody would actually look at Slater these days.

"Ech," Lisa goes.

"He could be cute," Jason says. He eyes Lisa. You can tell from his look that he doesn't like how she's being bitchy. "You just have to see underneath."

I wonder for a second why I'm not worried what people think of Jason being gay, but maybe not everybody knows, and anyway, you can't tell that Jason's different just by looking at him, the way you can tell a mile away that Katy and Slater are complete outsiders. Besides, Jason doesn't go around being the gay guy. He just goes around being Jason.

"So, why is Seth worried?" I ask Lisa, noticing that my shakes are back somehow.

"He gave out the alcohol," Jason says. Lisa nods.

I cross my arms to try and hide the trembling. "But I wasn't drunk."

"Well, that's good," Jason goes. And he's right. If I hadn't been sober, all of this would be worse. A lot worse.

"Even if I was drunk, it wouldn't be Seth's fault."

"I know," Jason says, arching his left eyebrow. "But still.

I'm glad nobody has to deal with that." I'm glad too.

"He's coming now," Lisa says. "Stop talking about him."

The hall's emptied out a little. I think I heard the bell ring a second ago, but I wasn't really paying attention.

"Hi," Seth says. He looks right at Lisa. "I totally heard you."

"It wasn't your fault," I tell him, while Lisa turns red. Seth looks sort of surprised. He glances at Jason.

"She wasn't drunk," Jason explains.

"Plus, they're saying there was a cinder block in the middle of the road," Lisa adds, recovering. "Right, Anna? Cameron was swerving to avoid it."

"A tree branch," I say.

"Your brother was really good Friday," Seth tells me.

"That's what I heard."

I won't tell them. I won't tell anybody, except maybe Ellen sometime ten years from now. I won't tell them that when we got out of the car, home from the hospital, Jack wouldn't get up off his hands and knees. That he wouldn't stop dropping earth into the grocery bag. That he was picking up a lot more soil and new grass than leaves, and that my mother talking to him softly and my dad jabbering at him and me wailing like some kind of animal wouldn't budge him. I won't tell them that my father finally had to pull my brother up by his armpits and drag him into the house.

They're all staring at me. Seth puts his hand out like he's going to touch my shield, but then he stops.

"Does it hurt?" he asks me.

"Just looks weird," I say. "And my eye waters a lot."

"It doesn't look weird." He pats my shoulder.

"Didn't the bell ring?" I ask them.

Jason gives me a ride home. We're quiet practically the whole way. I notice a bunch of books scattered all over his backseat. Something called *I Am* and something called *Tragic Sense of Life*. Also, there's *From Socrates to Sartre* and *Man and His Symbols*. I've at least heard of that one.

"You're into psychology?" I ask.

"Philosophy," Jason goes. I know exactly nothing about philosophy.

"So, how did you and Ellen get to be friends?" I hate silence. It always makes me think there's something wrong.

"I liked the way she says things," he tells me.

"You mean the way she plays with words?"

"No," Jason says. "Not that. That's annoying, to tell you the truth."

"What do you mean, then?"

"She just seems like she's actually thinking some of the time."

I kind of get what he's talking about, and I kind of don't. And I want to ask him if he thinks it seems like I'm thinking sometimes. Only, I already know that probably he doesn't see me that way, and for some reason it matters, and I feel embarrassed.

"Thanks for the ride," I tell him.

"Any time."

When I walk into our house, my father's Tumi suitcase is packed and sitting by the mudroom door. Everybody's in the kitchen. I know Rob probably gave Jack a ride home, only Rob's car isn't out front, and Rob isn't in here.

"What's going on?" I ask them. My brother takes a gulp of chocolate milk straight from the bottle.

"Use a glass," my dad tells him. My dad never comes home early from work.

"Jack's going to California," my mother says. "Will you be okay here alone for a few hours? We're driving him to the airport." My dad never lets anybody use his luggage, either.

"Why are you going to California?" I ask Jack. He takes another gulp, so my dad answers for him.

"Your brother wants to pay his respects."

"Oh," I say. "Should I go?" They all look at me. "Oh." I guess not. Jack grabs the Tumi handle. "Are you coming back?" I ask him.

"Wednesday or Thursday," my dad says. "Depending." Depending on what?

"You'll miss more school," I say.

Jack doesn't look at me. He wheels the suitcase though the mudroom and then lifts it down the three steps into the garage.

"Take care, Anna," Jack says finally. It's way worse than "Excuse me."

Two weeks after Jack and Cameron started going out, I was sick. As a dog. My father thought it was food poisoning, and my mother thought it was the flu. My dad yelled at me for eating the half tuna sandwich he'd left out on the counter, which he'd forgotten to put in the fridge after he wrapped it that morning. He shook his head with amazement that anybody would eat a tuna sandwich not cold from the refrigerator. It didn't help.

I was in bed with the wastebasket nearby, too wiped to get up, but thirsty and hot and miserable. And then Jack walked in.

"Hi," he said.

"Where's Cameron?" I asked. They'd been joined at the hip.

"Helping her mom shop for her little brother's birthday party. You need anything?"

"Huh?" I just wasn't used to him going out of his way to be nice. Even with how much more it seemed like he was trying with me since the summer. I was still suspicious.

"Do you need anything?" he repeated.

"Um . . . some ginger ale maybe. And crackers."

He left and came back five minutes later with a tray. "Provisions," he said, putting the tray over my legs. I smiled. At the beach, when we were little, we used to play sailor underneath the houses. We'd pack plastic bags of crackers and pretzels and butterscotch candies, and we'd have bottles of water. Those would be our provisions—we loved saying that word—and we'd fight pirates and sea monsters and starvation on desert islands.

"Thanks." I sat up a little on my pillows and took a sip. "It must stink in here."

"Kind of," he said. "Want me to open some windows?"

"Yeah."

He started with the one over my desk. The fresh breeze felt good. When he was done with the other two, at the head of my bed, he sat on the floor with his back against my dresser.

My cell rang. I grabbed it and flipped up the top. It was Ellen. It kept ringing.

"It's Ellen," I told Jack. He just looked at me. Normally I'd answer it and forget all about my brother. But there he was being so decent to me, so instead I snapped the top down and let the cell drop onto my bed somewhere in the covers.

"Jack," I said. "I'm not trying to be mean or anything." I took a sip of ginger ale. He waited. "But . . . why do you think Cameron went out with you, in the first place?"

He sighed and looked out the newly opened window. I knew what he was seeing: a telephone wire, that big maple tree, and the streetlight. He started humming.

"What?" I wasn't trying to be rude. I was really wondering about it.

Jack stopped humming. "Nothing." He shrugged. "But you are really superficial."

I felt my face get hot. "What's that supposed to mean?"

"Listen," he said. "You just implied that there's something about me that is lesser than Cameron." I opened my mouth to argue, but he kept talking. "That's what I mean. You think about things that aren't important. Like who's got more status than the other person." I started feeling nauseous again. "And you make your decisions about that based on things like clothes and friends and where people sit in the lunchroom and who people hang out with. And if people aren't just like you, you think they're not worthy and that nobody else who matters to you thinks they're worthy. And so you write those people off." I thought I might throw up. "I remember when you weren't like that. I remember when you cared about things that mattered and when you weren't always sizing everything and everyone up all the time. And I liked you a lot then." He stayed where he was, leaning against my dresser, butt on the floor, knees up.

He wasn't giving me that disgusted look. He didn't have that disgusted tone of voice. He was really talking to me. Trying to tell me something. I sat there a long time, feeling smelly and nauseous and awful. I didn't know what to say. I just sat there. And so did Jack. We sat there and sat there. My phone rang again. I rummaged around in my sheets and flipped up the top. It was Ellen again. I didn't answer it. We sat there some more.

"So, how old is Cameron's brother?" I finally said.

"Nine on Thursday."

"Does Cameron like him?" I asked.

"A lot," Jack said.

"Do you like him?"

"He's a cute kid," Jack said.

We got quiet again.

"What are her parents like?" I asked.

"Her mother's really hyper all the time," Jack told me. "But not like Dad. She doesn't have to have everything be a certain way, and she doesn't yell at the drop of a hat. She just hovers a lot."

"Hovers?"

"Yeah. Hovers."

"Maybe because she knows you two are in love," I said. "Parents worry about that, right?"

Jack smiled. That big, wide smile. The one I used to know really well, which looked totally the same on his face now as it did when we were little.

"Yeah," he said.

8

"I'M CALLING ELLEN," I TELL JASON AND SETH AND LISA. WE'RE
in the lunchroom.

"Again?" Lisa asks. "She's going to have about fifty messages
from you the first time she checks her cell." It's Tuesday. Ten
days since the accident.

"I don't think anybody would mind fifty phone calls from
their best friend after they've almost died," Jason goes. He
stares at Lisa with this look of his. It's not exactly a nasty look,
just one that commands respect. Lisa blushes and bites into her
pizza slice.

I dial the hospital number first. I've never gotten Ellen on that
phone, but a couple of times a nurse answered and told me Ellen
was too doped up to talk. This time it rings forever again, so I hang
up and dial her cell. Call number seventy-three or something.

"It's Ellen. Leave a message. If this is Anna, try me back in five minutes."

"Hi, Ellen. I'm sitting here with Lisa and Seth and Jason at school. We're missing you and we want you to call as soon as you're feeling up to it. I snuck in—sorry, *sneaked* in—to see you the other day, and you were in your new room with practically no tubes or machines, and somebody had washed your hair and you didn't look too bad, and I wanted to write you a note or something on your cast, only there was no pen anywhere. Anyway . . ." Lisa and them are looking at me like I'm nuts. "The Ashleys keep saying hi to me in the hall, and Kevin and Trace called to ask how you were doing, and then they broke up and then got back together again. Lisa's getting a Mac instead of a Dell, and we're waiting for you to get out of the hospital so we can start an SAT study group, and did you know that Seth eats a different candy bar each week, like all week, and this week's is Caramel Crunch, and I've seen him eat three already, and it's not even twelve thirty? And there's a rumor starting that Jason and Sleev-eth are going out, only Seth swears he's not gay, and Jason swears that even if Seth was gay, Jason wouldn't date him for a million dollars, which is an interesting question. The question being, What would we each do for a million dollars?"

I hold my cell out to everyone. "Anybody want to leave a message?"

Lisa takes the phone. "Anna is crazy, Ellen, but you must already know that. Get better! We miss you!"

She hands it to Jason. "The only way out," Jason says, "is to simply observe." Then he passes the phone to Seth.

"Get well soon. We need you for vocabulary." Seth hands the phone back to me.

"Bye," I say.

"The social worker at the hospital suggested we get some counseling," my mother tells me.

I'm in the family room, channel surfing. I'm used to having one eye right now, only I'm just a little worried it's making me bend my head in a weird way.

"You don't need counseling, though, right?" my dad adds. They've sat down on the L of the couch next to me. They never sit on the couch in here.

"I don't know," I say.

"I think it's a good idea," my mother says.

"Really?" I'm not even sure what counseling would be like. "Why?"

"Right," my dad tells my mom. "That's what I think."

"The social worker thinks differently," my mom says.

"Did the social worker suggest Jack get counseling?" I ask.

"She suggested it for all of us," my mother goes. "But especially for you and Jack."

"Dad doesn't think we need to, though," I say. "Right?"

"I don't really see the point," my father says. "We go through difficult times. We live. We learn. We move on."

"If she wants to go," my mother says to my father, "she'll go."

"Right," my dad says. "If she really wants to."

"Does Jack want to?" I ask.

"We haven't asked him yet," my mother says. "We're waiting until he gets back."

I stay quiet. I'll do whatever they tell me to do. But I don't really care.

"All right, then." My father stands up.

"I think we should talk about this more," my mom says. He makes this huge, exaggerated sigh.

"It's fine," I say to my mom. To keep them from arguing. To keep him calm. "I don't really want to go."

Besides music Jack loves movies. Films, he would say.

"We're not watching this," I went one afternoon, years ago, as soon as I saw words on the bottom of the screen.

"But it's a classic," Jack said. "It's *The Four Hundred Blows*."

I was too young then to make an obscene comment about that title. But I was old enough to know it wasn't going to be as good as the top countdown on MTV.

"It's in French," I said.

"So?" Jack argued. "The French make really good movies. Just give it a chance."

"Watch it in your room, then."

"My screen's too small in there," he told me. "You have to see this stuff on a big screen."

"Mom!" I yelled. "Jack's hogging the good TV again!" Which wasn't even fair of me, because we'd already made a deal about whose day was whose.

"Work it out," she yelled back from her office upstairs.

"It's Thursday," Jack reminded me. Thursday was his. We'd agreed.

"But the top ten is a special today," I complained. "This month's mystery host is going to be on." I wanted to relax before dinner the way I wanted to relax. I couldn't explain why exactly, but I was in a bad mood, and it mattered.

"That's not a special," Jack said. "That happens every month. And it's never a mystery anyway. It's whoever won last month's vote. Just watch this with me. You might like it."

I hated those old movies. I hated subtitles. They make you work too hard. I didn't want to work.

"If I wanted to read," I told him, "I'd get a book."

And then I went to my room, mad at him and mad at the small screen on my dresser and just mad.

Later, at the kitchen table, my father said, "So, tell me something you learned today, Anna." Ever since I'd woken up, I'd had a feeling he might ask that night. You never knew exactly when he would, but it had been a bunch of days. You always had to be prepared. Only somehow, no matter how prepared you were, it never went well.

"Fractions," I said.

"What do you mean, 'fractions'?" my dad asked. "There's a lot of different elements to fractions."

"I learned that if you add fractions, you have to find the same numerator."

My father was serving himself rice. He stopped with the serving spoon in mid dump. "I hope you didn't learn that," he said.

My brain started blinking. "That's what we learned." I was pretty sure I was right, even though my father was already making it seem like I was wrong.

"I hope not," my father said. "Think about it." He put the serving bowl back down on its hot pad.

I felt my mind go fuzzy. "If you add fractions, you have to find the same numerator," I said again.

My father placed his fork on his plate, wiped his mouth with his napkin, and glared at me. "Why are you repeating the same incorrect information?" He had that irritated tone of voice. The tone that comes right before the mad one, and the yelling.

"That's what we learned," I insisted, only now I wasn't so certain, and the fuzziness got fuzzier.

"Harvey," my mom said.

"Think about it again, Anna," he ordered. "Put down your glass, straighten yourself up in your seat, and take a minute to think."

So I put down my glass without drinking, and then I couldn't think at all. I was sure I had it right. I remembered learning it and practicing it and planning that it was what I would say if he asked the question that night. Only, now it wasn't right.

"I'm thinking," I said. Was it a trick question? "But that's what I learned."

"She meant denominator," Jack mumbled.

"Why?" my father asked him. Jack looked down at his plate. The vein in my father's temple pulsed. "Why do you do it?"

Jack kept looking at his plate. I was so thirsty.

"You could see that I was trying to help Anna figure something out for herself, couldn't you?" my dad asked, only it wasn't a question. Jack looked up at him and then back down again. "Why did you interfere?" With my dad looking at Jack, I figured it was safe to pick up my glass. I did. I drank.

"Is this really necessary?" my mom tried. But Dad never listens to her.

"Well, what did you learn today?" my father asked Jack. "Since you're eager to share what you know."

I took another drink, glad he wasn't on me anymore.

"I learned that sometimes a script is better if there's not very much dialogue in it."

My father stared at Jack. "What?"

"Did you ever see *The Four Hundred Blows*?" Jack asked. "I learned that less dialogue is better from watching *The Four Hundred Blows* today, plus from watching some other films this week and thinking about it a lot."

"You watched another movie?" my dad said. "What have I told you about watching all that TV?"

"It wasn't TV," Jack said. "And I did my homework first."

"Did you watch it on a TV screen?" my father asked him. Jack nodded. "Then, it's TV."

"No," Jack said quietly. "It's not."

"Don't argue with me," my dad said. So Jack shut up.

I don't recognize the number on my cell caller ID. But I answer it anyway.

"A million dollars?" Her voice is soft, and the edges of it don't quite meet.

"Ellen!" I yell. I'm sitting in front of the TV on the L-shaped couch in the family room, not doing my SAT prep handbook.

"The problem with a million dollars," she tells me in that voice, "is that after taxes it's really only half a million." She still sounds like her, only way, way tired.

"Ellen!" I yell again. I picture her, sitting up maybe, in her hospital bed, a tan phone pressed to her ear.

"And half a million dollars really isn't that much money these days."

"How are you? How's your lung? How are your ribs? How's your leg?"

"My leg is really heavy. My ribs and the place where they had the chest tube is brutal if I laugh. I made this funny nurse leave this morning."

"Does everything hurt that much all the time?"

"Not so much. Painkillers."

"You drug addict."

"Yeah."

"You sound dreamy," I tell her.

"That's about right," she says.

"Everybody's asking about you all the time. Have you seen all the cards and stuff?"

"Yeah," she says.

"The bear is from Jason."

"Isn't it weird how much like Whitey it looks, only bigger?"

"Totally."

"Isn't Jason so cool?"

"Totally," I say again.

"I wish he wasn't gay."

"I know."

"How are you?"

"I don't know."

"How's Jack?"

"I don't know."

"Did your father have a conniption?"

"I don't know," I say. "You're fading."

"Yeah," she says. There's this silence. I can hear her breathe. Then she goes, "Ten million. Ten million would be a different story."

"Ten million?" I ask.

"I'd probably do just about anything for ten," she says, and suddenly I know for sure what Jason was talking about earlier. She's got this thinking tone of voice. This tone where she's taking an idea seriously, turning it over in her mind. Paying attention. "Yeah," she goes. "Anything. Except kill, injure, or molest somebody."

"I did that for free," I go, before I even realize what we've just said.

And then I start crying. So hard I don't make a sound. There's this long silence while I lose it. My SAT book slips off my lap and thunks onto the floor. "Are you still there?" I finally manage to choke out.

"Hmm, Anna," she says, and then I think she falls asleep.

9

WEDNESDAY NIGHT. ELEVEN DAYS SINCE I KILLED CAMERON.

I sit on the L of the couch and try to study. I have a biology quiz tomorrow, and I need to get a good grade on it. It's hard to focus. I mean, my right eye can't focus, obviously, because of the drops to keep my pupil dilated, but my brain has no excuse. *The key to speciation is reproductive isolation.* I've written it in my spiral, circled it, and starred it, so it must be important. I open up the textbook and try to find *speciation*. *The key to speciation is reproductive isolation.* Ms. Riffing gives us rhymes to help us remember. She puts tunes to them to help us more. She's a great teacher, and even though I don't like biology, I love her class. *The key to speciation is reproductive isolation. The key to speciation is reproductive isolation.* I hear my mother's footsteps on the third-floor stairs, heading down. I look at the clock. Twenty minutes have passed, and I don't know what the hell I'm reading.

"I can't concentrate," I tell my mom when she walks in. She sits on the edge of the couch.

"You're not worried about it, are you?" she asks. I don't know what she means by "it." Failing the quiz? My eye? What?

"A little," I say anyway.

"There's nothing to worry about!" That's my father, yelling from his spot at the kitchen table. It's where he likes to play poker online. He sets up his laptop and plays for hours. His favorite game is called Texas Hold 'Em. He plays for real money. He has a rule for himself that he's not allowed to keep playing if he loses more than a thousand dollars in one year. I don't know what he does with the money he wins. I don't even know if he ever wins. I just hear him cursing a lot and yelling at the screen.

"You're worried about Ellen, too, I guess," my mom goes.

"And other stuff." Things I can't say out loud to her because I don't have any practice saying anything important out loud to her. Like, *I killed somebody. How do you make the fact of something like that go away? How do you make the fact of something like that not nag and poke at you, like some kind of virus that's stuck in your blood, stuck in your cells, stuck in who you are and who you will be forever?*

"Would you leave her alone, please?" my father shouts from the kitchen again.

"I'm not bothering her," my mother calls back. "We're talking, Harvey." She says *talking* as if it's a word my father doesn't know the meaning of. Then she looks at me. "I'm not bothering you, am I?"

"Amanda!" my father yells while I shake my head. She's not bothering me exactly, but then again, I'm not used to her trying to talk to me so much either. We both hear my father stand up and start walking toward the family room.

"Well," she says, "come upstairs if you want. I'll be in my study." I never go up to the third floor. I think the last time must have been when I was about ten.

I hear her pass my father in the hall on her way to the stairs. She hisses something at him, and he snaps something right back, and when I can tell he's resettled himself with poker, I get off the couch and go up to my room.

I sit cross-legged on my bed, staring at a sheet of white stationery edged in silver. I'm trying to think of what to write to Cameron's family. I can't think of anything beyond *Dear Mr. and Mrs. Polk.* After that I just start to hear screaming, stopped, and I'm shaking so hard I don't think I could write a word anyway.

So I stand up and cross my arms tight and pace the room. I make three laps back and forth before the shaking slows down. I land in front of my mirror.

"Listen, Jack," I say to my reflection. My curls are tied back in a mass of metallic spirals, and my skin is so pale it's almost the same shade as the stationery. I don't have to wear the spaghetti strainer at home unless I'm sleeping, so I can see that my eye is almost back to normal except for a greenish tint to the skin around it and my enlarged pupil. "I can't believe that . . ." I stop. That sounds too fake or something. Plus, I never knew the left side of my mouth twitches when I talk. Ugh. "Jack," I say again, trying to keep my mouth moving evenly. "When I was driving home that night, I had no idea . . ."

I shut up and watch my reflection give me the finger. "Try it again, and come up with something decent," she tells me.

"Look. Jack," I try again. "You must be feeling . . ."

But it's too hard. How are you supposed to put into words something so awful there are no words for it at all?

I do a search on the Internet. There's a lot of sites for if you're dying. They give you links and medical information about what happens if you have this kind of cancer or that kind of heart condition, and what medications and operations you can have and your chances of getting any better. A bunch of other sites are for if someone you love dies. They're about mourning and grief. I read some of them, and it seems like nobody really knows all that much about it, even though they all have a lot to say. If you're mourning, it's like there's no rules about what you're supposed to feel when, or for how long. Sometimes you feel better if you can talk to other people who are also mourning, and sometimes that makes you feel worse. All the postings seem really confident, like they're the ones with the right answers, but then the next one will just as confidently say something totally different. I try to decide how much I'm mourning Cameron, and it's hard to figure out. She wasn't my sister, or even my friend really. I don't think I miss her exactly. It's more like I'm horrified every time I think of her, and I feel this dread and guilt that's a part of that ink in my blood all the time.

I think about forwarding some of the grief sites to Jack where he would see them out in California, but then I'm not sure if I should. So I don't. Instead I keep searching. These other sites come up about if you want to die. Some of them tell you all the reasons why you shouldn't commit suicide. Because you'll go to hell, which is worse than whatever you're unhappy about here on Earth. Because other people will be hurt and will miss you. Because it's wrong. Because you don't really want to die, but you just want help to feel happier. Then other sites tell you exactly all the different ways you can kill yourself. They tell you about the best way to hang yourself, the most effective method to slash your wrists, which pills to take if you're serious about dying. I don't like those sites. They make me nervous. Besides, I don't want to commit suicide.

Mostly I want to find out what you're supposed to do when you've killed someone else. What you're supposed to do for all the people who really loved her. And also what you're supposed to feel.

But I can't find any sites about that.

If I were Jack, I'd probably create one. Except I'm not him. I'm only me.

Somehow I fall asleep, and it feels like I've slept for hours, only when I wake up, on top of my comforter, the clock tells me it's forty-five minutes later.

I can't fall back asleep, and I can't concentrate on anything that requires my brain, so I decide maybe I'll clean. At least you don't have to think when you clean.

My parents collect glass. Blown glass. They have vases and paperweights and sculptures all over the house. I'll go around and dust them. When they're totally clean, the pieces by our windows change colors with the light somehow. Most of the them have a lot of orange and red in them. But the newer ones have more blue and purple. They're kind of cool.

I get myself downstairs and into the kitchen, rummage around underneath the kitchen sink, and find a relatively clean rag and some Windex.

My father doesn't say anything, but he does start to shuffle his real deck of cards while he stares at the laptop screen. He shuffles like a professional, making the cards whir and jump and fan without even looking at them.

"God damn it," he mutters. Then he starts to hum.

I start in the living room, where the most fragile pieces are. Spray and wipe. Wipe and spray. They're not so dusty to begin with, but I can tell they look better after I've gotten to them.

"What are you doing?" my dad finally calls to me.

"Cleaning," I tell him. I notice that if I slow my hand to stop a rag over the glass, my hand buzzes just the littlest bit, as if it were resting on the sill of a moving bus or train.

"Cleaning the glass?" my father asks.

"Yeah," I say. I imagine him cutting his deck of cards over and over and tapping at his mouse.

"Remember when Jack broke the bud vase?" he calls.

We were ten and eleven, and we were playing indoor baseball. That's when you pull the pom-pom off the tip of a knit cap, you make chair cushions the bases, and the fireplace is home plate. You bat with your palm, and you use ghost men. It's a good game when it's raining out, or when you're bored at night. We weren't supposed to be playing it because of the glass.

I was up. I smacked the pom-pom over Jack's head. He had to turn to chase it. I ran like mad to first and slid off it toward the blue armchair cushion for second. Rounding that, I slipped on the wood floor and grabbed at the window seat, trying to stop myself. The bud vase went down. And shattered.

"God damn it!" my father yelled from somewhere in the house. We heard his feet pounding the hallway above and then pounding the stairs. "That better not be glass!" He charged into the living room and saw us stuck, frozen. His face was pink. He scanned the room, taking in the cushions, the pom-pom lying innocently in the corner, the fragments of glass, like a kaleidoscope exploded.

"Did you do this?" he asked Jack. Instead of answering, my brother took a step forward and half leaned down. I stood very still, hoping my dad wouldn't ask me if I had done it.

"Stop," my father said. Jack straightened up fast.

"I was going to clean it up," he tried to explain. I held my breath, waiting for my turn.

"You don't clean broken glass with your hands," my father told him. "What is the matter with you?" Jack stood still again. My father stared at him, jaw muscle jumping. "What is the matter with you?" he said again. "I want an answer!" Jack stayed quiet. "What is the matter with you, Jack!"

"I don't know."

I started breathing again. Maybe my dad wouldn't notice me as much as Jack this time. You never knew.

"Harvey?" My mother had arrived at the living-room door. "Oh." She stared at the shards on the floor. She looked around the room, checking the paperweights and vases and sculptures. "The bud vase?" she asked.

My father pointed at Jack. "Don't just stand there. Get the broom and the dustpan." But then, before Jack could move, my father said, "What were you thinking?" Jack didn't answer. "What were you thinking?" my dad asked again. His eyes were wide open with lots of white showing, like the Black Stallion, upset. Jack stayed quiet. "I'm asking you a question, Jack. What. Were. You. Thinking?" That vein in his forehead started hopping.

"Harvey," my mother said. "Calm down." I inched toward

the door. I wanted to get to the hall, the stairs, my room. Away from my dad, away from his making you feel stupid and wrong.

"I'd like to know what he was thinking!"

Tears began to bloom out of Jack's eyes. My mother's mouth set itself into a thin line. She couldn't do anything. I inched farther.

"Stop it," my father said. He hates crying. "Stop it now." Jack's tears didn't stop. My father shook his head and snorted through his nose. "Get the broom."

About an hour later Jack banged through my closed door and marched right up to me. I was leaning against two pillows on my bed, braiding beads into my hair and trying to stay invisible. He was sweaty and tearstained. He didn't say a word. He just punched me hard twice in the arm. Really, really hard.

"Dad," I call back into the kitchen. I tuck the Windex under my arm and shake out the wet rag. "Jack didn't break that vase."

I hear him drum his fingers on top of his deck. "Okay."

"Okay?" I stay where I am and keep talking loud so he'll hear me. "Did you just say 'okay'?"

"Anna, I'm in the middle of a game."

"But what does 'okay' mean? Did you know that he didn't break it?"

"I don't know. Probably. I don't really remember."

I walk over to stand in the kitchen doorway. He's got his feet up on the seat of a chair and his laptop propped on the lazy Susan, which is so old it doesn't spin anymore. "Why did you punish Jack and not me?"

He sighs and keeps his eyes on the screen. "I didn't punish Jack," my dad says.

"You yelled at him," I remind him.

"Yelling isn't punishing," my dad says. I can see his eyes moving across the screen.

"Yes, it is." I know that what I'm saying is true. I'm sure of it.

"No." He taps his mouse and looks up. He lifts his glasses to rest on the top of his head. They get buried in his hair. It looks stupid. "Yelling is just being angry. Punishing is giving a consequence. Like docking allowance or TV."

"But you made him stay and help you clean it up, and you didn't make me."

"I remember both of you helping to clean it up."

"I didn't help."

He lowers his glasses. "Anna, please. This isn't a good time for either of us to have this sort of discussion. Understand?" He looks down at his deck of cards and then back at me. I can see him working to keep the irritation out of his voice. "You're trying to have a quiet night after a difficult week. I'm trying to also. I'd like to play some poker. Do we have to have this conversation?"

"You brought it up."

"No, I didn't."

"Yes, you did. You said, 'Remember when Jack broke the bud vase?'"

"Fine," he smiles a strained smile at me. "Okay. But now I want to go back to my game." He clicks himself on and drops one of his legs off that chair.

"Yelling is punishing," I tell him.

"Hmm," he goes, scanning the screen. On it clusters of cards pop up, surrounding a green poker table.

"Dad," I say. "Yelling is punishing."

10

JACK GETS HOME WHILE I'M IN SCHOOL ON THURSDAY. WHEN I
see him, he's not as blank or stiff as he was before. He's sitting
cross-legged on his bed, clattering away at his laptop.

"Writing another movie review?" I ask him.

"Yeah." He doesn't stop typing while he's talking.

"What's it called?" I ask.

"*Eternal Sunshine of the Spotless Mind.* I watched it in the hotel."

But I'm not really interested in his movie review. "How was
the funeral?" What a stupid question. How was the funeral?
How about, *It sucked, Anna.*

"In the words of Cameron's little brother," Jack says, looking
up, "not what I expected." And then he goes back to his keyboard.

It's almost dinnertime on Friday. I'm in the Gersons' downstairs
guest room waiting for Ellen to get home. I took her pillows and

comforter and her stuffed animals and vanity table and all her clothes and the little round crystal hanging in her window and her TV and everything from her bedroom, and I tried to set it up exactly the same down here. And I fixed up the guest bathroom. I took all her grapefruit shampoo and conditioner and kiwi bath oil and body scrub and arranged them by the sink along with her Sonicare toothbrush. I set up her crutches by the bed, and I'm just wondering how she's going to shower with the cast on her leg, when the Gersons wheel her in.

"Surprise." I give her a hug. Which, as I already know, is hard to do when one person's in a wheelchair.

"This looks terrific," Mrs. Gerson tells me, meaning the room, and then she and Mr. Gerson leave, saying something about getting Ellen food or ice chips.

"Wow," Ellen goes, looking around. She's way pale. There's a scab on her cheek where that bandage used to be, and her hair seems longer.

"You lost weight," I tell her. She's pretty thin to begin with.

"Yeah. Hospitals are great for that." She eyes my shield.

"You like it?" I ask her.

"You look like C-3PO." It could be worse.

"I brought homework and movies and ingredients for chocolate-chip cookies, or we could call Jason and those guys, and they said they would come over."

Ellen closes her eyes for longer than a blink and then opens them. "Actually," she says, "I'm pretty tired."

"Oh," I go, feeling stupid.

She wheels herself over to the bed. "I kind of want to take a nap."

"All right."

"Um," she goes. "I'm sick of my mom. Could you help me?"

She shows me how to help lift her from her chair onto the bed. Her leg is heavy and clumsy. We have to sit her on the edge of the bed first and sort of lean her back. Then I have to lift her cast up after the rest of her. She winces and her face grits itself in pain.

"Aagh." I think it's her ribs more than her leg, but I'm not sure, and I don't know what to do. Ellen does, though. She lies still for a bunch of seconds, and then her face relaxes. "Thanks for remembering Whitey." She picks up her polar bear. She's had him on her pillow since she was born. He's all worn out and gray looking now. She rubs him across her chin. "Thanks," she says again, yawning and then immediately wincing. About a minute later she's asleep.

I wake up to my own voice. I'm making this moaning, calling sound. It's still coming out of my mouth as my light snaps on, and then my father and Jack are standing at the foot of my bed.

"Stop it, Anna," my father's saying. "Stop it now."

My blankets are all over the place. The back of my tank top is sticking to my skin. I'm shaking. The eye shield is falling off. My mother rushes in.

"Anna?" She sits on the edge of my bed and puts her hand to my forehead.

"She had a nightmare," Jack says.

"You're all right," my father tells me.

"She's trembling," my mother says.

"She's fine." His gray hair is in complete bed head. He touches my sweaty shoulder. "You're fine," he says again.

"I'm fine," I say. My father leaves, and Jack snaps off the light. You can still see, though, from the light in the hallway.

I'm in my room, not on Ocean Road. I'm in my room, not in the street with Ellen in my lap and a ponytail, sharp as glass, in my eye. I'm in my room, not out in the middle of the road, huddling near Jack, who's huge as a giant, tree trunk legs planted wide and firm, tree limb arms and branched hands raised up and out. I'm in my room, not in the darkness with policemen and screaming, stopped. I'm in my room, I'm in my room, I'm in my room.

"I need water," I say. Jack gets it for me. I wait, the shaking slowing down while my mom sits close.

"Thanks," I tell Jack after I take a swallow.

"You're welcome," he says.

There was this one night, back when we got along. That year's beach house was called Porpoise Swim. I had run into my room to pull on jeans and a sweatshirt, even though it was so hot out. I hate bug spray and won't use it. I could hear my family's voices clear as anything as they trooped down the stairs from the upper deck, under the house, and out to the driveway.

"And then they cut to something else," I heard Jack saying, "and then they slice up her eyeball, only it's a special effect, so it's not really her eyeball."

"That's disgusting," I heard my mom go as I pulled the hood of my sweatshirt up. Mosquitoes will get your ears if they can't get anything else.

"Really, it was a cow's eye, except you couldn't do that today because of animal rights and all," Jack explained. It sounded as if they had reached the bottom of the stairs. "You never heard of it?"

"No," my mother said.

"But it's famous," Jack told her. "They're showing it at the museum next Saturday. Could we go home a day early so I can see it?" I walked down the hall toward the great room.

"You know we don't leave until Sunday," I heard my dad say. Then he went, "Is that dripping?" He meant the outdoor shower underneath the house, where we were supposed to rinse the sand off before we came upstairs and inside. It was always dripping. "Damn it," my father said. "It is."

"Yeah, but it would just mean leaving one day early, and you can't rent it." It sounded like they were almost at our driveway. I stepped out onto the deck through the sliding glass doors.

"We're not leaving one day early so you can see *Anderson's Dog*," my father said. I could see the flashlight beams bouncing around out near the street. "Anna!" my dad called as I stepped onto the top stair.

"It's *Andalusian*," I heard Jack say. "Not *Anderson's*."

"Turn the shower all the way off when you come down!"

My father had been standing right there looking at it. Why couldn't he have turned it off?

"Whatever it's called," my father told Jack, "we're not driving back a day early for it."

They were all the way out of our driveway and down the street by the time I got to the dripping shower. I could see them stepping in and out of one another's shadows. I reached for the little blue on-off wheel, bent down, and twisted it to the right. And in that exact moment there was this flash of light and something hit me hard, and then I was on my back on the sandy ground at the edge of where the driveway began and the underneath of the house ended. A crash of thunder. More lightning streaking the sky. Another bang. And then driving rain.

By the time Jack and my parents were back under the house with me, I was sitting up, moving each arm and leg one by one to make sure I wasn't half dead, or something. My heart was pounding. I couldn't believe that a second ago I had been leaning under the dripping shower, and now I was sitting all the way over here. I couldn't believe how fast it had happened. How I hadn't even had time to scream.

"I think I just got hit by lightning," I told them. They were soaked.

"What?" My father was frowning at the exposed stairs, probably trying to figure out how to get up them without getting more drenched.

"I mean," I said, "I didn't get hit exactly, but my hand was on the metal thing for the shower. Maybe lightning hit the house and it went into the metal, and since my hand was on it—"

"Anna, I'm dripping wet," my father said. "What are you talking about?"

"Mom," I said. I thought I was okay. Nothing hurt exactly. "I think I got electrocuted or something."

"Are you all right?" she asked.

"I don't know," I told her. "It was really weird."

"Can you move everything?" my father asked. He'd finally looked at me.

"I think so," I said.

"Are you burned anywhere?" He walked over and touched my head, my arms, my back. My mother looked too, over his shoulder.

"I don't think so," I said. He stepped away and began squinting at the rain and the stairs again. "But it knocked me all the way over here."

"Anna, it couldn't have knocked you that far. Come on, now. Don't exaggerate."

"I'm not," I told him. "It really—"

"I'm making a run for it," my father interrupted. My mom glanced at me and followed him up. Jack stayed where he was.

"Did you really get electrocuted?" he asked.

"I swear," I said. Why didn't they believe me? I don't make up stuff like that.

"What did it feel like?"

"Like you tackled me."

"Really? Let me see your hand." We both looked at my hand. Maybe it would be black. But it wasn't. "You were just touching this?" Jack asked, and he pointed to the blue on-off wheel.

"Yeah," I said. "Right when that first big lightning happened."

"Cool."

"It kind of scared me." As soon as I said that, I started to cry, which was embarrassing.

Jack looked away while I pulled my fist across my eyes. He waited awhile before he said anything. "Are you okay?"

"Yeah." I sniffed.

He watched me finish sniffing. "Maybe you'll end up with special powers."

"You mean like a superhero?" I asked.

"Yeah." He walked to the space underneath the deck, where there was more height. "Like that. See if you can fly."

"I can't fly." I followed him.

"Just see." He made a scoop out of his hands, lacing them

together, palms up, and locking them. "I'll give you a boost."
So I backed up to him and stepped my right foot into his scoop.

"One," Jack said. "Two. Three!" He threw me upward, and
I leaped and fell right back to the ground.

"Nope," I said.

"Nope," he said back. "It's still cool."

"Do you think I'm okay?"

"Yeah. You're fine."

"What's Andalusian?" I asked him. He thought about it.

"I forget," he said. "Either that, or I never looked it up in the
first place."

After they leave, and it's dark in my room again, and I'm sipping from the water Jack brought, I think about all that. I don't
know why exactly. But I remember how it felt like I'd been hit
by a truck, and I remember how scared I was when my parents
didn't get it. And how Jack didn't mind that I cried, and then
made that step for me out of his hands to see if I could fly,
even though we were both too old to really believe I would. I
don't know exactly why I'm thinking about all this, except it
has something to do with how Jack brought me the water just
now. He filled it three-quarters full so it would be enough, but
not so much that I'd spill, and he waited to let go of his grip
on the glass until he was sure I had it firm in my shaking
hands. He was the one in the nightmare trying to stop something terrible from happening, and he was the one in real life
double-checking that my hand wasn't blackened, burned to a
crisp, and letting me feel scared without minding.

11

JASON AND SETH AND LISA AND I TAKE TURNS MAKING SURE
Ellen gets to and from classes okay. She'll be in her chair for at
least another two weeks, and she moves really, really slow. When
we're just sitting around, Jason massages Ellen's earlobes.

"That feels so completely amazing," Ellen goes every time he
starts. You can see just how amazing in her face, and I don't
think it's only because she has such a thing for him. Her eyes
and her cheeks and her whole face and neck relax.

Sometimes, out of the blue, she'll wince, as if someone's hit
her, and then she'll hold really still for a few seconds.

"It's not my leg so much as the ribs," she tells me the third
time it happens. "And especially by my boob, where that
goddamn chest tube went in."

Technically I'm supposed to be wearing my strainer in

school, but I'm not following that particular rule anymore. Yesterday at Dr. Pluto's I had a gonioscopy. He put some sort of special contact lens in my eye and then vised my face and used the slit lamp to look at things. The blood was totally gone, he told me, and the tear was tiny and basically healed. I have to take atropine—that's the drops to keep my eyes dilated—for a few more days, and then I'm done.

"I'll see you in a week," Dr. Pluto said, palming my head.

Now Ellen and I are making our pathetic way through the humanities hallway. The only problem is, the armful of helium balloons Lisa tied to Ellen's chair keep popping and startling us, which is a pain in the ass, plus if Ellen jumps, her face grits itself in pain and she has to hold still for a while before she can move or talk or not look like she's dying.

"Lisa's not around, right?" Ellen asks.

I take a quick glance up and down the hallway, which is pretty crowded. "Yeah," I say. "I think she turned left for Spanish."

"Okay, stop," Ellen says. We stop. "Let's just pop the rest of these." There's three left. She pulls at one of the strings so she can reach a balloon. I pull at the other two.

"Got a pen?" she asks. I hand her a pencil. She stabs a few times, but the pencil is dull, the latex is tough, and Ellen's stabs are weak, I guess because of her ribs.

"What about a nail file?" I dig one out of my backpack side pocket. "Here." I stab at a red one, and it pops. A couple of kids jump.

"Excellent," Ellen goes. "I mean, no offense to Lisa. But do another one." So I pop another one. Some other kids yelp. Ellen starts gnawing on the strings.

"Wait, wait," I go. "Let me untie them." So she lets them go, and I start to untie. I'm good at that, actually. Any time somebody's chain gets knotted, they ask me for help.

"It's freezing," Ellen says.

"You're always cold," I tell her.

She yawns this huge, loud yawn and then winces. "Ow."

"You okay?" I ask.

"I'm just really tired. And then it hurts to yawn."

"It's your first day back," I remind her.

"I know," she says. "I just didn't think I'd be so tired."

She doesn't sound good. "Do you want to go home?" I ask. It's not like anybody's going to stop her. The teachers are being pretty nice to both of us. I can't remember the last homework I completed. And I've failed two tests and a quiz already—that biology quiz, actually—and everybody's let me take them over.

"Mostly it's that I keep thinking about Cameron," Ellen tells me. "You know?"

"Yeah," I answer. Only, I can't stand to think about it, so I say, "Can I pop the last balloon?"

"Go ahead."

I pop the last balloon. A few kids jump, and this one girl screams a very loud, very long scream, and the second she stops, I make this gasping sound, and then I think I'm going to vomit, only I don't, and I'm shaking so hard I drop my backpack, and Ellen's asking what's the matter, and I can't get my mouth to work, and Ellen's grabbing my hand and asking why it's all sweaty, and my heart is pounding and I think, *Oh, my God, I'm having a heart attack, but sixteen-year-olds don't have heart attacks,* and Ellen's telling me to stand up already, just stand up, and our biology teacher walks by and she's going, "Girls? Are you all right? Girls?" and she stays with us while I get my breath back and get my heart to slow and while Ellen sinks lower and lower into her chair with her eyes closed and these tears just sliding out of the corners and down her cheeks, and then Ms. Riffing checks with the junior-class vice principal and then calls Ellen's mom, who says we're like soldiers battling shell shock and we should both go right to bed, and drives me home.

Instead of getting into bed, I'm sitting at my desk, staring at the cover of my history book. I hear Jack's step, walking into the kitchen from the mudroom and then on the stairs, and he stops at my door. He takes the earphones out of his ears. I can hear squawking coming from them. I swear he's going to be deaf before he's twenty-one.

"Your friend Jason told me you and Ellen freaked out in the hall today before sixth period," he says. He needs a haircut, and he has this line between his eyes I've never noticed before, and the whites are sort of bloodshot.

"Did people see?" I ask. But I don't really care.

"I guess," he says. "Jason seemed pretty worried. That guy Seth was with him. They both went out of their way to find me."

"Oh," I say.

"They seem pretty cool, those two," Jack tells me.

"Oh," I say again.

"Do you want to go to Top Hats?"

"With you?" The idea of going anywhere with Jack is so strange I can hardly picture it.

"Yeah," he says. "I'm sick of being cooped up in this house."
Even though he just got home.

"How would we get there?" I ask.

"I heard Mom drive in when I was walking upstairs," he says.
We still have only one car. The Audi. "We could tell her we'll
pick up Dad from work." They're going to buy another Honda.
They're not sure if insurance will cover it, and my dad's been
yelling at a bunch of people over the phone about it.

"I'm really behind on my homework," I tell Jack.

"Bring it," he says. "I'll bring my laptop. We can hang out
there until dinner."

In the garage he hesitates on the third step from the mudroom. "Who's driving?" he asks.

"You," I tell him.

Dr. Pluto warned me that outside during the day without the
shield my eye may be sensitive to the sun. This is the first time
I'm trying it, and he's right. As soon as we're out of the garage,
I have to cover the eye with my hand. I haven't dug up my sunglasses yet. So I have to keep my hand there until we're inside
the diner.

I order onion rings and a Coke. Jack orders fish sticks and a
Diet Coke.

"Gross," I say about the Diet Coke. It's not like he's got a
weight problem. "How can you drink that?"

He shrugs. "I like the taste."

The waitress comes over to refill our water glasses, even
though they're still about half full. "Where's your friend?" She
remembers Ellen and me from when we used to come here all
the time.

"She broke her leg," I say.

"Same time you broke your eye?" the waitress asks.

"Yeah," I say, and I guess something about my face makes her stop asking me about it. Instead she goes, "This your boyfriend?" Jack snorts Diet Coke out his nose. Nice.

"My brother," I say. Jack's wiping himself off.

"Should have guessed," the waitress says as she walks away. "You two look alike."

It reminds me of when Cameron said that, and I wonder if it reminds Jack, too, when he sticks his earphones back into his ears and taps his iPod and won't look at me. Which makes me start to shake again. My wrists mostly, stuttering on the edge of the table.

"Jack," I say.

He picks up a fish stick, dips it in ketchup, and then puts it back on his plate.

"I just wanted to tell you that—"

"Don't," he interrupts.

"But I never really—"

"Don't, Anna!" he goes again, and he thumbs his iPod, scrolling up the volume.

I reach over and try to pull an earphone out of his ear. "After the accident I thought you—"

"Stop it!" He whips his head up and away from my hand. His face is thin. Like Ellen's. It's filled with that disgusted look, that one that tells me how unbelievably small I am.

"Okay." My chest is filled with ink. "Let's just go home."

I've barely even started my onion rings, but I put a twenty on the table, grab my backpack, and walk out. Jack's right behind me. He slides into the driver's side as I'm snapping on my seat belt one-handed so that the other can cover my right eye. Jack starts the car and smacks the CD player on, turning up the volume on some band he must love. After two seconds of driving I turn the volume way down. He turns it back up. It's a good ten minutes before I notice we're not going anywhere I recognize.

"Where are you going?" I ask. We should be home by now.

"Nowhere," he says.

"Why are you so mad?" I ask him.

"Why are you such a bitch?"

It digs this big black hole right into my gut, and there's nothing to say back. I just sit here, feeling inky and heavy and horrible, while Jack keeps driving.

"Do you even know where we are?" I ask.

"No," he says. Great. He takes an exit, and we start passing gas stations and fast-food restaurants.

"What music is this?" I ask.

"Spoonerism," he tells me.

"Spooner what?"

"Spoonerism."

We sit here and listen.

"Did Cameron like this song?"

"Yes. Shut up. I'm not talking about her with you."

"I wasn't trying to get you to."

"Yes, you were." He pulls into a gas station.

"No, I wasn't."

"You're full of shit," he tells me, easing the car up next to a pump.

"And you're being an asshole."

"I'm fucking *sad!*" he explodes at me. "Do you understand?"
And he leaps out of the car and starts walking. Just walking.
He's headed for the road. The gas station guy is pumping gas.
I don't know what to do. I have only five more dollars on me
and no credit card. My parents don't give us our own. And
Jack's walking—more like slamming—away down this street,
and it doesn't look like he's turning around anytime soon.

"Stop," I tell the attendant. He's pumped three dollars. He
stops. I get out of the car and pay him. I have to take my hand
away from my eye. I try to close just the right lid against the
light. It's hard to close just one lid. I end up sort of squinting
both eyes instead. The attendant gives me the change. And
then I run after Jack. It takes me a good few minutes to catch
up to him. For one, it's hard to run with a hand over your eye.
But also, I'm wearing these slip-on shoes with no back, plus
I'm not exactly an athlete.

"Stop," I huff at him when I finally catch up.

He keeps walking. I'm out of breath and wiped out. I have to
half jog to stay near him. I drop my hand and go back to squinting.

"Jack."

"What?" he says. I'm right on his heels, like a dog being
walked. I reach out to grab his arm.

"Come on," I say.

He stops, curses, kicks the ground, and turns around. His
face is like a mask. Like one of those painted demon masks you
see from Africa. All big, wild eyes and stretched-out, gaping
mouth and insanity. I take a big step backward, away from him,
and cover my right eye with my palm again. We stand here staring at each other.

"Somebody's going to steal the car," I tell him finally. It's still there, with the key in the ignition, by the pump. "We've got to pick up Dad."

Jack must hear something in what I've said that makes his mask shift a little. He bends down and grabs a handful of thistle and pebbles and dirt, and he hurls it. He grabs another handful and throws that, and then another one. He's crouching, and cars are driving by, and I still don't know what to do. After a few more grabs and throws Jack stops but stays crouched. He puts his head in his hands, and I don't think he's crying, but I kind of wish he were, because somehow that would be easier than this.

"I don't want to deal with Dad," Jack says. "I do not want to deal with Dad."

He wipes his face with his hands.

"You've got dirt on your face," I tell him.

He stands and starts walking toward the car. Then he stops again, and I nearly run him over, I'm so close behind. I could have damaged my eye all over again.

"I can't stand this," Jack tells me. "Seriously, Anna." He nods, as if I've said something to agree with him somehow, and then he starts walking again.

When we're pulling out of the gas station, I turn his music on for him. I turn it up really, really loud. He changes the CD from Spoonerism to some other band. I close my eyes against the brightness. It's all I can do not to cover my ears now. Partly because the music is so unbelievably loud, and partly because it sucks. Instead I tuck my hands under my thighs and grit my teeth. I stay like that, eyes closed, hands jammed, jaw locked, all the way to the bank.

12

"THAT'S EASY," LISA SAYS. "LIKABLE. EXTRA LIKABLE."

We're at Ellen's studying for the SATs, which are totally screwed up this year. Instead of being on the first Saturday of December, like always, they're the Saturday before Christmas. So that gives everybody two extra weeks of anticipatory agony. Because at my neurotic school, people start studying early and worrying earlier.

"Popular," Seth says. He's sitting next to me on the floor at the coffee table in Ellen's living room. He's half concentrating on what the rest of us are doing and half writing something on a piece of paper he's hiding underneath his thigh. Every now and then he rubs his calf on my ankle. I try to see what's got him so interested on that piece of paper.

"*Charisma* means 'popular,'" he repeats.

"It's more than that, though," Jason says from the couch next to Lisa. "Right?" He's asking Ellen because it's the sort of thing she would know. "Doesn't charisma have something else to it?"

She's been getting quieter and quieter since she got home. Not as quiet as Rob, but noticeable. At least, I can tell Jason's noticed. He's always making a point of directing what he says to her. Maybe to get her into things again. I don't know.

She's sitting in the wheelchair with her leg propped on an ottoman right next to the coffee table and a huge chenille blanket wrapped around her shoulders. We've got a bunch of markers out, and every time we review a word, someone makes up a sentence with it and then writes the sentence on Ellen's cast. The word has to be in a different color than the rest of the sentence. So far we've got *Ellen's cheeks are* gaunt *from the shitty hospital food* and *The pornographic cable channels present* tawdry *options for the masses,* and a few more like that.

Ellen shrugs at me and Seth. "What do you guys think?"

Seth looks up from whatever it is he's working on underneath his leg. "I thought charisma had to do with how people look, too," he says. "Don't you have to be hot to be charismatic?"

"Read the definition," Jason tells Ellen. Seth pulls a Tootsie Roll out of his pocket, unwraps it, pops it into his mouth, and then picks up the bowl of sour-cream-and-onion potato chips and passes it to me. I grab a bunch and pass the bowl to Jason. It goes around the circle while Ellen reads. Seth rubs my ankle again. I rub back.

"'A personal magic of leadership arousing special popularity or enthusiasm.' That's One. Two is 'a special magnetic charm or appeal.'"

"But people who are charismatic are always good-looking," Seth insists.

"I thought we just disabused ourselves of that," Ellen says.

"Disa-what?" Lisa asks her.

"Proved ourselves wrong." Ellen sighs.

"Whatever." Lisa leans back onto the couch in a huff. I don't blame her. Who but Ellen would know a word like *disabuse*? The SAT people, I guess.

"So it's not attractiveness," Ellen says, holding the bowl and then not taking any chips. "It's some other thing. Some other quality. Like . . . like . . ." Then she shrugs again and gives up. Before the accident Ellen was not a shrugger. Or a giver-upper.

"Weirdly sexy?" Jason offers.

Ellen perks a little. "Yeah," she says, and she sort of straightens. "Think about it. Who are the most long-lasting celebrities or politicians? Some of them are objectively hot. But most have this weirdly sexy thing happening. Charisma." We all sit there and think about it. It seems sort of true.

"That girl in those frozen-dinner commercials," I say. Everybody nods.

"Bono," Lisa goes.

"They're not pure good-looking," Ellen says. "But they're weirdly sexy, and they have that magnetic charm and appeal."

"But just because you're good-looking doesn't mean you have charisma," Jason says. "That's the point."

"Cameron," I say. I've been thinking it since before Ellen even read out the definitions. Everybody gets quiet. I look over at Ellen. She nods and stares at her cast and then at the dictionary. She kind of sags, like a balloon, deflated.

"Let's do a sentence with her," Lisa says. "Anna, you write it."

Lisa hands me the box of markers she was holding. I look at all the colors for a while, trying to decide. I end up choosing black.

"Do you have a sentence?" Seth asks. I'm not sure. I sit here, the tip of the marker poised over Ellen's cast. It trembles, so I pull it away and cap it while I think. Everybody's waiting. "Cameron," I finally write, "= charismatic." It's the first sentence I've done today. The lines are jittery and wavery. They're strange next to Lisa's bold, curvy letters and Seth's wiry chicken scratch. It makes me not be able to look at Ellen, or at any of them, for some reason.

"That's not exactly a sentence," Lisa finally says.

"'Without the desire to see there is no seeing,'" Jason tells her.

"And that means what exactly?" Lisa goes.

Jason arches his left eyebrow. "It means shut up."

My cell rings. I toss the marker onto the coffee table and flip up the phone. "It's my mom."

They wait politely, smashing open a bag of baked corn chips, while my mother talks. She says I need to get someone to drive me home to pick up the Audi to drive to the car dealer on Bateson Avenue to pick her and my dad up because the new Honda they were supposed to buy today got accidentally given to someone else.

"Can't Jack do it?" I ask my mom.

"We called you first," she says. "You're closer than he is. He's at Rob's."

"Rob's isn't that much farther," I say.

"Anna, please."

"Why is the Audi at home?" I ask. "Why don't you or Dad have it?"

"We miscommunicated," my mom explains. "I thought Jack was taking it, so I got a ride with Phyllis. Your dad thought I was taking it, so he got a ride with Russell."

"I'm in the middle of studying," I say.

"Anna, this isn't an option. We're stuck here," my mom says.

"Is she giving you a hard time?" I hear my father ask in the background.

"I can't—," I start to tell my mother.

My dad gets on the phone. "Get over here now," he says. And he hangs up on me.

"What's the matter?" Seth asks. "Your teeth are chattering."

"No, they're not," I say. They all look at me funny.

"Can someone give me a ride home?"

Seth does. I have to direct him because he's never been to my house.

"Are you okay?" he keeps asking. I keep nodding behind my sunglasses. I'm going to need them for at least a few more weeks. Even though I stopped using the drops a couple of days after that gonioscopy.

"What happened on the phone?" Seth tries.

"Nothing," I say. "My mom just needs me to pick her and my dad up." I pull my arms around myself, and he drops it.

"So, what was that piece of paper you were so interested in at Ellen's just now?" I ask him. My teeth are chattering, and it's not even that cold out.

"My next big thing," he says.

"Your what?"

"My next big thing." He grins. He has sort of a goofy grin. "You need a big thing every now and then," he goes. "To keep life from getting boring." He reaches into the pocket on his door and grabs a Tootsie Roll.

"Here," I say. "You're driving." I unwrap it for him. Instead of holding out his hand, though, he opens his mouth. I ignore that and toss the naked Tootsie Roll into his lap, so that he has to fish for it. "So, what's a big thing?" I ask him.

"My first one was in seventh grade," he says, rolling the candy between his front teeth. "You know that huge water-wheel moat thing by the library?"

"Yeah," I go. "The one somebody made into a bubble bath about four yea . . ."

He's rolling and smiling.

"Oh my God," I go. "That was you?"

More rolling. More smiling.

"What about the colors?" I ask him. "That started later, right? Like, a year later?"

"Food coloring," he goes. "My favorite was the purple."

"Mine too!" I go. "How did you not get caught? I mean, they could have arrested you or something."

"Yeah," he goes, tucking the Tootsie Roll into the side of his cheek, making a little bulge. "Life without parole."

"Don't make fun of me."

"Never." He chews and swallows. "I'm glad you don't have that robot eye anymore during the daytime," he says as he turns onto my street. My arms have become uncrossed somehow, only I'm shaking again, so I recross them.

"Because I've been wanting to kiss you, only that thing was messing up the physics of it."

"The physics?"

"Who have you gone out with, anyway?"

I cross my legs now too. "Nobody," I say.

"I thought you and Paul what's-his-name were a thing."

"No," I say. We're around the curve now, almost at my drive-way. "He liked me, but I didn't like him back."

"Why?" Seth asks. I don't really know why. He was cute and cool, and he played soccer, and Ellen thought I should like him. "And what about Rothman?"

I roll my eyes. "Rothman is ridiculous," I say. "Here." He pulls into my driveway. I unknot my limbs and get out of the car. I try to seem calm while I make myself walk around to his side.

"Why do you like me, Seth?" I ask through his rolled-down window.

"Am I ridiculous if I don't have a reason?"

I shake my head. He reaches out and pulls a curl. And doesn't let go.

"Let go," I tell him.

The truth is, I've been kissed by only two guys. Paul what's-his-name and Rothman, and I've never really had a boyfriend, and I'm sort of old not to have ever had a boyfriend, and it's embarrassing and the idea of dealing with it all just makes me shake, only I've been shaking for weeks anyway, so maybe it's hard to know exactly what the shaking is about.

"Lean down," he says, keeping gentle hold of my curl.

"You never said what your next big thing is," I tell him.

"Lean down," he says.

"I'd really like to know."

"Lean down," he says again.

"I didn't say you could kiss me," I tell him. He keeps hold of my hair.

"Lean down." He's like a broken record. "I'm going to kiss your other eye."

I lean down. He lifts himself through the space of the window and very gently raises my sunglasses.

"Hmm," he goes. And then he very, very gently kisses my left eye.

"See ya," he says, and he's out of here. I'm shaking and shaking and shaking.

I get to the end of my block. That's how long it takes before I lose it. Chest leaping, body shuddering, sweating like I'm running a marathon. *Something happened to me in the accident,* I think as my slick palm slides all over the steering wheel. *I got injured somehow that nobody realized. My heart got hurt, and now I'm having a heart attack.* I manage to weave the Audi over to the side of the road and pull out my cell phone. I call 911. I stumble out of the car and think I'm going to vomit on the street, only I don't. I collapse onto the pavement, but by the time the ambulance gets here six minutes later, I'm almost fine, and Mrs. Caldwell is sitting with me in that navy blue sweatsuit with the white stripes up the sides.

"She was in a car accident about a month ago," Mrs. Caldwell explains to the EMTs. So even though they don't see anything obviously wrong, they decide to take me to the hospital. Mrs. Caldwell picks up my parents at the Honda dealership and drives them home. And Jack is at the house by then, and my whole family drives to the hospital in the Audi to get me, and I'm fine.

On the way home again, Jack and I sit in the back, with my parents up front, and it's like a trip to the beach, because when else are we all in the car together these days? My father's humming. Jack's got his earphones in and turned way up. I can hear that squawking sitting next to him. My mother keeps twisting around with this concerned expression.

"Okay, look," my father says finally. I tap Jack and nod at the back of my father's head, at his mass of gray hair. Jack pulls out his earphones. But then my dad doesn't say anything else.

13

SETH AND JASON AND LISA BRING TWO MOVIES OVER TO ELLEN'S.
Her mom has to go into her room to wake her up about three
times before Ellen finally wheels out with her hair messed up
and the same sweatshirt she wore yesterday.

"We got them both off Rosebud Is a Sled," Jason tells her.
"They're in Jack's top fifty list." I flop onto Ellen's couch next
to Seth. He puts his arm across my shoulders while we look.

"*My Life as a Dog*?" I say, looking at one of the DVDs. "What
is that? My brother is so weird."

"*Big*," Seth says, crunching into his Toffee Crisp and reading
the title of the other movie. "Which one should we watch
first?"

"*My Life as a Dog* will make you cry," Ellen's mother informs
us, walking through the family room to get to the stairs.

"Out, Mom," Ellen tells her, loud, and then she winces. Her ribs and the spot where her bra strap meets the cup must still really hurt. It creeps me out to think a tube poked right into her body there. I've seen the aftermath, once, when Ellen changed her shirt in front of me. It's all this gauze and white tape and a wettish spot in the middle. She has to change it twice a day. Ugh. Poor Ellen. I saw her laugh at something Jason said at school earlier, and then immediately grit her face and almost cry.

"I never weep at movies, Mrs. Gerson," Seth is saying now.

"Weep?" Lisa goes.

"Am I allowed to respond?" Mrs. Gerson asks Ellen.

Ellen shrugs. "A-parent-ly."

"That movie will make every single one of you cry," Mrs. Gerson announces. Then, at Ellen's look, she speeds up, saying, "Yes. Yes. I'm going."

So we watch *Big*. Seth keeps his arm around my shoulders the whole time. Ellen doesn't even seem to notice. I stick my tongue out at her to make her notice.

"Mature," she says out loud to me, but not like she cares.

"Shh," Lisa goes.

Later I can tell that Ellen's not even paying attention. Once, I see her eyes on the TV screen, but they're all spaced out, and another time she's braiding the tassels on the scarf around her neck.

Jason's not into it either. He wanders around the Gersons' bookshelves halfway through and pulls out something to read. When the movie's over and everybody's getting ready to go, Lisa starts teasing him.

"Since when are you such a bookworm?"

"That movie sucked," Jason says.

"Are you kidding?" Seth goes. "That movie rocked."

Jason slides his book back onto the shelf, using his body to hide it so that we can't tell what it was.

"What were you reading?" Lisa asks.

"You'll never know," Jason tells her.

"I can't believe you actually sat here and read a book while we watched a movie."

"Anna's walking me out," Seth announces. "Don't follow us. We're going to be fooling around."

"If you're lucky," I tell him, but I follow him to his car. We get in, and he leans over to kiss me.

"Don't," I say.

"Oh." He sits up straight again. He looks bummed. I'm not really sure why I stopped him. I want him to kiss me, but when I think about him kissing me now, I think about us kissing later, and us being boyfriend and girlfriend, and I get tired. And then I think about Ellen and how tired she is all the time, and how, truthfully, she's seemed not okay somehow, and I get more tired.

"So why did you come into the car with me?" Seth asks after a while.

"Because I like you," I tell him.

"Oh."

"It's just . . . there's a lot going on." I'm not really sure what I mean.

"Cameron?" It's the obvious thing.

"I guess," I say.

"I know." He looks at me sideways. "Did you see her?" At first I think he means did I see her car swerving. But then I realize he means did I see her dead.

"What kind of question is that?" I ask him.

"I just . . . ," he starts.

"Does it matter if I saw her?" Does he only like me because I'm some sort of reverse celebrity now? Because I'm some story?

"Anna. Whoa. I didn't mean to . . ."

"Does it matter if I saw her!" Does he think he gets status if he can go and tell everybody all the gory details? "Seth!" I'm shouting. Really shouting. "I'm asking. You. A question!"

He looks like I've just smacked him. "I was only . . ."

"Forget it," I tell him, opening the car door. "Just forget it."

The others are gone when I get back inside. Ellen and I set up our sleeping arrangements in her temporary downstairs room. Actually, I set things up, while Ellen watches and rubs Whitey across her chin over and over. She gets the bed, obviously. I sleep on the blow-up mattress, inside a sleeping bag.

"I saw which book Jason was reading," Ellen goes after we've turned out the light.

"What was the book?"

"The Bauble."

"The what?"

"Think about it, Anna."

"I'm not in the mood to think. Just tell me."

She sighs. "The Bible."

"Oh."

"Yeah."

"Is he religious?"

"I have no idea."

"He's into philosophy, you know."

"I know. And stealing."

"What?"

"He didn't put it back. The Bible."

"He didn't put it back on your shelf?"

"Nope."

"But we saw him put it back."

"It's not there now."

"Are you sure?"

"Yeah."

We're quiet, and I think she's almost asleep, but she's not.

"Let's not tell anyone," she says. "Okay?"

"About Jason?" I go. "Of course not."

"It's a weird secret to keep for someone," Ellen says. "You know?"

"Yeah."

"That they were reading the Bible."

"Yeah."

"That they stole a Bible."

"Right."

"But he definitely didn't want us to know he was interested in it. And he'd never tell something we wouldn't want him to tell, you know?"

"Yeah."

"Besides," Ellen adds. "Nobody in my family's going to notice a missing Bible anyway."

We're quiet again, and this time I'm sure she's asleep, only I'm wrong.

"Did you and Seth have a fight?" she asks.

"We're not even really going out to have had a fight."

She's too smart to buy that. "What was it about?"

I feel how wide awake I am. "The accident."

"How could you have a fight about that?" Ellen asks.

"We just did." Then it doesn't seem fair not to tell her more. We tell each other everything. "He wanted to know if I saw Cameron dead," I say.

"Oh," Ellen says. "Did you?" Coming from her, it doesn't seem like such a bad question. She was there too. She got hurt too.

"No," I tell Ellen. And I can hear the screaming, stopped. I shiver and zip the last part of my sleeping bag to get warmer.

"I'm sorry I passed out," Ellen says.

"What?"

"I'm sorry I passed out." Her voice is sort of breathless, like she's been on a StairMaster or something. "I was thinking that I escaped the worst of it by passing out, and you were on your own."

"No," I tell Ellen. "No way. I never thought of it like that. No."

"I've been sort of thinking that."

"You nearly died," I say, and I concentrate on not starting to cry. "I only got some stupid blood in my eye. Plus, I was driving. I could have done something different."

"I might not have passed out like that if I hadn't been so drunk."

"Even if you hadn't passed out, there's nothing you could have done." I hear her smacking her pillow. She can never get her pillow the way she likes. She's always smoothing it or plumping it or something.

"Were you terrified?" Ellen asks after she settles things with the pillow.

I think about it. I try to think about it the way she would. The way Jack thinks I should, the way Jason likes for people to do. I really think about it.

"I'm more terrified now," I say.

I'm on Ocean Road and there's a glass ponytail slicing into my eye, and there's the earth dangling above me in the dark sky, and there's screaming and screaming and screaming, and there's Jack, giant size, with tree trunk legs planted wide and tree branch hands up and out like a good monster traffic cop's, and there's a tidal wave of salt water and blood about to destroy us, and there's screaming and screaming and screaming, and then the screaming stops.

"Anna, wake up!"

The lights are on. Mrs. Gerson is shaking my shoulders. "Anna!"

"I'm awake," I say. My heart is going wild.

"You're soaked," Mrs. Gerson says. "Soaked." I don't know who she's talking to. I look over at Ellen, half sitting up in bed.

"Are you okay?" she asks me. I touch my face. It's wet. My heart is like a little animal trapped inside my chest.

"Did I wake you up?" I ask. My body is shaking again. From tip to toe. My whole body.

"You could say that," Ellen says sarcastically.

"Was I really loud?" I ask them. *A tidal wave and my brother and screaming, stopped.* I could vomit.

"Freight trainish," Mrs. Gerson says. "Get up, now. I'm running you a bath."

"A bath?" My heart starts to slow down.

"Mom, you can't make her take a bath," Ellen says. The shaking turns more into a slow shudder.

"For God's sake, Ellen," Mrs. Gerson goes.

"It was just a nightmare," I tell her. "I'm okay. Really. I don't need a bath." But actually, a bath sounds sort of good.

"You are not okay," Mrs. Gerson tells me. She looks at Ellen. "And neither are you." She leans over and kisses Ellen's head and then touches her cheek. When Ellen shakes her off after a second, those tears sliding out of the corners of her eyes, her mom sighs at her in this nice way. Then Mrs. Gerson turns to me again, takes my hand, pulls the twisted sleeping bag off my legs, and tugs me to a stand. "Neither of you is okay."

14

I DON'T KNOW WHAT MRS. GERSON SAID TO MY PARENTS, BUT IT'S a week later, Thanksgiving is in five days, and Jack, Ellen, Mr. and Mrs. Gerson, and I are all on a plane to Florida. We're going to some resort "to get away and recuperate," as Mrs. Gerson puts it.

"Isn't it weird," Ellen's saying to Jack, "how Anna and I have been best friends for years, and you and I have barely ever said a word to each other?" Her back is to the window and her leg is stretched out in my lap. That cast is heavy. We got to board first because of it, and we'll get off last.

"Same with Anna and Rob," Jack answers. He's across the aisle from us.

"That's only because Rob never talks," I say.

"He talks," Jack says.

"Barely," Ellen goes.

"I hate peanuts," Jack tells us, holding his mini package of them by the edge.

"Since when?" I ask him.

"Since always."

"I didn't know that," I tell him. "I hate peanuts too."

"So does Mom."

"Ellen loves them," I say. "Give her yours."

Jack gets his own room. Ellen and I share. There's a pool with purple and red tiles checkered around its sides and a swim-up bar where you can buy drinks and sandwiches and chips. The beach and ocean are through a gate and down a stone path. There's a huge, round floating trampoline anchored beyond the breakers pretty far out. We never had that when we were little. It looks like fun.

The Gersons keep their distance from us, except at dinnertime, when we all go out to eat. They let us order wine, and I notice Ellen motioning the waiters to fill her glass every time it gets near half empty. Other than dinner, when they pass by us, Mrs. Gerson makes either a shooing motion or else puts up her hands, as if we're throwing eggs at her.

"Recuperate," she orders. "Recuperate."

Mr. Gerson brought a Monopoly game, which I never would have thought of, but we take it from him and set it up by the pool. We arrange things so that Ellen can prop her leg in the shade but sunbathe the rest of her. She still has a jumbo-size square gauze bandage underneath her bikini where the strap meets the cup, but it's not as bad as it seemed a few weeks ago. It's smaller and cleaner now. She and I make Jack shuffle over every twenty minutes so we can stay in the sun and maximize our tans. When Jack and I get hot, we jump into the pool and then come back to shake our wet hair onto Ellen. We cover her leg with a cut-out piece of blue tarp to protect the cast. We all bought sunglasses in the airport. The wire-frame-with-colored-glass kind. Ellen bought a shade of light blue. Jack bought orange. I think his are weird, but Ellen says they're funky and cool. So whatever. I'm working on trying not to worry about things like that. I bought as dark a pair as I could find. My right eye still hurts when the sun hits it. Ellen and Jack and the mirror tell me that the pupil's dilated, only not to the degree it was before. Also, it's not round so much as vertically oval. All I know is Dr. Pluto said not to worry, and I'm allowed to swim.

"Seventy-eight entries," Jack announces right after his turn at Monopoly. He's been taking his laptop with him everywhere. Since UCLA's deadline was so early, and since you can use the same essay for different schools, he's pretty much through with college applications. Deadlines for NYU and Brown aren't until January anyway. So mostly he's not working, but check-ing his Web site and the Cameron link. "Two new ones today." He means memorial posts for Cameron.

I roll, land, and then go directly to jail.

"I thought that one written by Shelly was really nice," Ellen tells Jack. I didn't know she'd gone to the site.

"Did you write one?" I ask her.

"Didn't you see it?" she asks me back.

"Ellen's was great," Jack tells me sort of softly. I try to think of a quick lie, but my brain won't work fast enough.

"You've looked at the site, right?" Ellen asks.

I shake my head. Ellen rolls the dice and gets really busy moving the hat.

"I'm hot again," I say to Jack. "Want to jump in?"

"It's just weird," he tells me. "You haven't even looked?"

"Hotel," Ellen tells Jack. Then she winces. "Aaagh."

Jack and I have gotten used to seeing her pain come suddenly. It's the chest tube wound, mostly. Her ribs aren't as bad. We've learned to wait it out with her. So now, within a few seconds, she relaxes and hands him some of her colorful cash. He hands her a little red building in return.

"You haven't even looked at it?" Jack asks again. I stare at the red and purple tiles in the pool and feel small.

"Not yet," I say.

It's a wave made up of tree branches, millions and millions of them in all shapes and sizes, and it's bearing down on me, and somehow it's clear water, even though it's tree branches, and I can see my father behind the wave in the distance, and I can tell he's just hurled the wave at us, and I look around for my mom, but I can't find her to help, and there's screaming and screaming and screaming, and the wave is rising and curling, all those tree branches interwoven and meshed together, and the screaming and screaming, and a jagged glass ponytail splashes out of the tree branches and latches on to my eye, and then Jack is next to me, feet planted wide, hands up and out, and I know he'll be able to save us, and he's shouting loud, "Stop, stop," but the wave keeps coming, and it's the screaming, it's the screaming and screaming and screaming that stops.

I sit up fast, my heart racing, and my stomach rising into my throat and mouth and then falling again, and I'm breathing really loud, and it's dark, and then something hits me, and it's Whitey, the polar bear.

"Ellen?" I say. I fumble for my lamp and turn it on. She's half sitting up, which is actually sort of how she sleeps these days anyway. She's got the phone in her hand.

"Don't call anybody," I tell her. My entire body is shuddering.

"What's the nightmare?" she whispers.

"Don't call your parents." My heart starts to slow. "Come on. It's embarrassing."

"What's the dream?" she asks, hanging up the phone. I swallow to get the sour taste out of my mouth.

"It's just a bad dream." I peel off my nightshirt. An extralarge T that says TALK TO MY AGENT across the front. Ellen got it for me as a gag last Christmas. Now it's wet with sweat.

"Nice apples," Ellen tells me. My heart's regular now, but my curls are matted to my skull.

"Apples?" Underneath the damp sheet I wiggle out of my sweaty underwear. "You are so weird."

"What's the dream?" Ellen asks me again.

"What do you think?" I ask her back. She slumps deeper into her covers. "I'm sorry," I say right away. "I'm sorry." I toss Whitey back to her, but gently. She rubs him across her chin with one hand and starts plumping her pillow with the other.

"Do you ever dream about it?" I ask. I move to a cooler, drier spot in my bed. It feels better.

"No," she says, pounding and smacking. I like the sound. "I just dream that I'm a mermaid mummy."

"A mermaid mummy?"

"Don't tell anybody."

"I won't."

"In the dreams my torso is all taped up in this tight gauze and my legs are fused together, and I'm on land, and I can't move."

"Oh."

She smushes and whacks a few more times.

"Tell me when you're ready for the light off," I say.

She tugs and flattens. "Leave it on," she goes. So I do.

"Your friend Seth called," my mother says over the cell phone. "He says he's had trouble reaching you."

I unfurl a towel with an underwater scene on it. "I'm not picking up when it's him," I tell my mother. Ellen shakes her head, and Jack gives me the thumbs-down. We're in the hotel gift shop. It's drizzling outside, so no pool or beach this morning.

"What should I tell him if he calls here again?" my mom asks.

"Just don't pick up when it's him," I say, rolling the towel back into a sausage and returning it to the shelf. "Check the caller ID." Ellen picks out a seashell anklet and gestures for me to put it on her good ankle.

"Oh, Anna, I'm not going to remember to do that every time I pick up the phone."

I get Ellen to hold the cell to my ear while I lean down to clasp the anklet on. "Do I have any mail?" I ask. Which is a ridiculous question. What mail would I have?

"No," my mother says. "But your teacher Ms. Riffing called to say that she can work with you after school to catch you up after Thanksgiving."

I stand and take the phone back from Ellen. "Are we going to Buck and Jerry's?" That's my uncle and aunt. Jerry is a woman.

They don't have any kids, and we usually spend Thanksgiving with them.

Jack's holding a huge conch shell. The kind you blow into to make a sound like a horn.

"We'll see," my mother says. It's what we do every year.

"What do you mean, 'we'll see'?" I ask her. Jack holds the conch to Ellen's ear. She smiles. They get along pretty well. They went for a walk alone the other day. Well. A walk and a roll. "Rock and roll," Ellen said later. I was napping, and when I woke up, they were gone. Not that Ellen can get so far. I felt left out and uneasy, which is stupid, I guess. But I couldn't help it.

"We'll see if we're all up to it," my mother says. "Dad was suggesting we just stay home."

"I don't want to stay home," I say. Now Jack has the conch up to my ear. I can hear the ocean on one side and my mom's faint breathing on the other. The idea of what she's saying makes me nervous. Just the four of us, home together having dinner on Thanksgiving? Alone?

"Well, I'll tell Dad that."

"Is he there?" I ask, moving away from Jack and the conch. I'm surprised I've asked, because I never talk to him on the phone when I'm away. She puts him on.

"Hi," he says.

"Hi," I say.

"Are you kids going to buy anything?" the saleslady goes. Which, if you ask me, is pretty rude behavior for a fancy hotel. We all ignore her.

"See any porpoises?" my dad asks.

"Not yet," I say. "Can I go hang gliding?"

"Absolutely not," he says. "Are you using sunblock?"

"Yeah."

"What number?"

"Fifty," I lie.

"Put your brother on the phone."

I hand the phone to Jack. He hands me the conch.

"Hi," Jack says. He waits a second. "Yeah," he looks at me. "We're fine."

Ellen's been napping a lot. A whole lot. But now, for some reason, she's getting stir-crazy. When I walk out of our bathroom, she's sitting in her wheelchair in front of my queen bed, holding up her dad's car keys. Rental-car keys.

"What are those?"

"You know what they are," Ellen goes. "Come on. Take me for a drive."

Jack's in his room watching movies or maybe listening to music.

"I'm not in the mood," I tell Ellen. "Besides, your parents will kill us. How did you get those, anyway?"

"They always leave them in the bottom of their pool bag," Ellen says. "I fished them out this morning. Come on." She jangles them at me.

"Are you crazy?" I say. "If something happens, your dad could be liable for a ton of money."

"Nothing's going to happen." Ellen tosses the keys in my direction. I let them fall to the floor, while she winces.

"Please?" Ellen goes a few seconds later. "I can't swim or anything. I'm bored out of my mind."

"All right," I say. "If we get Jack to drive."

Ellen gives me a long look.

"What?" I say.

"I want to go, just you and me."

"You don't like Jack?"

"You'd rather I didn't like him, but that's not it."

"What do you mean, I'd rather you didn't?"

"You wouldn't want him and me to be friends. But that's a different subject. You're changing the subject. Anyway. It's not that. I want you to drive." She starts to wheel herself.

"I'm not changing the subject," I say. "You brought it up. And how come you want me to drive?"

She pauses at the hotel dresser and grabs her white, floppy hat.

"I just do," she goes, adjusting the hat on her head, wincing with how it hurts when she raises her arms like that, and then gliding her chair across the room.

"I don't care if you and Jack are friends," I tell her, even though now I'm not sure if that's true.

"Good," she says. "Don't forget your sin-glasses." She's got the door open, only it's one of those heavy ones that close on their own, and it looks like it's about to smash her, so I have no choice. I scrape the keys up off the knobbly rug, snatch my shades off the bedside table, and grab the door from Ellen.

"I feel kind of sick," I say, following her out into the hallway.

"You'll feel better once we get outside," she tells me. But I don't. I feel worse in the elevator and way worse in the hotel lobby.

"It might be heatstroke or something," I worry as we pass

by doormen, or porters, or whatever they are, and rock and roll outside.

"Come on," she says. So we keep going. In the parking lot Ellen eases herself into the backseat. I fold her chair, which takes me less than fifteen seconds now, lift it into the trunk, and then slide behind the wheel.

"I feel really sick," I tell Ellen. Maybe I'm going to throw up. My hands are jiggling on the steering wheel. I can't drive. There's no way I can drive. Ellen waits for more than a minute while I sit here shaking and sweating. Then she gives up.

"I knew it," she says, and I can see her face in the rearview mirror, completely disappointed.

15

THE SUN COMES OUT, AND IT'S LIKE IT NEVER EVEN RAINED, so we go to the beach. We always pick a spot far from the water and close to the path because it's nearly impossible to roll a wheelchair on sand. I carry all our stuff.

"I'm going to swim out to the trampoline," I tell her when we finally settle.

"Do you feel up to it?" she asks.

"I'm fine now," I say. And I am. "It must be something I ate."

"But that was just a few hours ago," she points out. "If it was something you ate, wouldn't you still be sick?"

I swim out, wearing my sunglasses. It's a long way, and I'm breathing hard by the time I reach the ladder. I hang on to it for a while before I even try to climb up. There's nobody else here, even though it's big enough to fit about ten adults comfortably.

All along the rim is this rubber bumper, I guess so you only go over the edge when you really mean to. I can't figure out how the thing is anchored so far out, so deep. But it is.

For a minute I think about jumping, but I didn't check out jumping with Dr. Pluto, so I wave at Ellen and then just lie flat and feel the sting of the sun on my face and belly.

Then I hear giggles, and two little kids monkey up the ladder. A brother and a sister. About nine and ten. Nut-colored hair, eyes, and tan. I scoot over to the side bumper of the trampoline. They start jumping right away.

"Higher!" the girl screams. "Higher!"

"Watch this," the boy goes, and he falls on his butt and bounces up to his feet.

"Higher!" she screams again.

"Look," the boy goes. "You can make it spin!" and he starts running around the bumper edges, which makes the trampoline spin in place. She follows him. I sway to the side a little when they get near, and they do a little hop so they won't run right into me.

"Faster!" she yells. "Faster!" They've got us spinning in the water pretty fast. Then the boy stops.

"I'm going to push you in," he tells the girl.

She shrieks. "No! Jeremy! No!" Before she can get in another no, he's scampered right to her and shoved her over the edge. I can hear her shrieking a beat after she disappears. Then I hear a splash. Jeremy grins at me, holds his nose with one hand, and then leaps off after his sister.

Two minutes later Jack climbs on. "Did you see those kids?"

"Yeah," I say. "Cute."

He doesn't jump. He lies on his stomach, leaning up on his forearms so that he can stare out at the horizon. "Ellen said you got sick or something."

"Yeah." The sun has me sort of dopey. "I feel better now."

I roll over onto my stomach. The plastic of the trampoline smells like seaweed. It's warm and damp under my right cheek.

Jack gazes out at the water.

"See any riptides?" I ask him.

"No," he goes.

"Good."

My father was cursing and struggling to get the umbrella raised. I looked around for my mom. She was already on her raft, swimming out to brackish green infinity. On calm days she would even bring a book out there with her. She likes true stories about survival adventures. Mountain-climbing accidents and shipwrecks and campers lost. Sometimes she'd float so far out, the lifeguards would stand up on their white towers and start whistling and waving their arms at her. Then she'd have to paddle closer in. But today was too rough for books. My mom had her hands full just paddling out past the breakers.

"Hey," Jack said, squinting at the lifeguard tower to read the squiggled-chalk report on swimming conditions.

"Don't drop the chairs like that," my dad said, finally clicking the umbrella's canopy into place. "You'll break them."

"Dad," Jack said. "Mild riptides today. It says so on the board." He pointed.

The lifeguards sat up pretty high, white zinc on their noses, with dark sunglasses, orange swimsuits, and binoculars dangling around their necks. They were always blackly tan, with maybe some white peel spots on their shoulders or faces. They posted the water temperature and the time of high tide each day in white chalk on the board. And they wrote up warnings of small riptides. If the rips were really bad, the lifeguards spiked red flags up and down the shoreline. It was against the law to go into the water if there were red flags out.

"I don't want you throwing down our chairs," my father said, ignoring Jack and letting his fall to the ground. He spotted my mom and waved his arm at her as he walked into the surf. She was facing land, so she probably saw, but she didn't wave back. She paddled herself sideways and then around and headed straight out to sea.

About an hour later Jack and I were in the breakers, trying to stop the ocean without much luck. Every now and then, when we drifted to the left, I could feel a mini riptide. They don't let you make any progress when you try to swim or walk back to shore. Even if land is just a few feet away, the weight of the current keeps you from moving. When people drown, it's because they get so tired fighting. They see the beach is only an arm's length off, and they keep swimming straight in and getting nowhere. Then they exhaust themselves and that's the end.

But my dad had taught Jack and me what to do in a riptide. As soon as you realize you're in it, you let it take you out to sea. It's counterintuitive, my dad explained, meaning it doesn't make sense to your gut. But if you let the tide pull you out to its triangle tip, even if you're really far out, then all you have to do is swim parallel to shore until you're beyond the rip's boundaries. After that you can swim straight back in to land.

It's important not to panic, because panicking makes you tired. And it's important to pace yourself. That's what my father always said.

"Hey," I called to Jack, only he wasn't there. He'd timed things wrong on the last wave and was tumbling underneath the water somewhere. *Dad looks weird, doesn't he?* That's what I was going to say. Because he did look funny. Off somehow. *He's in a rip,* I thought, and he was. Right in the middle of a small, dark triangle with ripples on the surface, like scales on a fish, going at an angle against the rest of the ocean. He was swimming and swimming and swimming and getting nowhere. There were surfers all around him, in every direction, but they were on their boards on the surface of the water, skimming above the current.

"Dad!" I yelled. Only he was too far away. And Jack had wiped out all the way back to shore. I spotted him sitting on his butt in the undertow, getting his bearings. I looked back at my father. He was still trying to swim. He was working hard, shoulders straining.

"Hey!" I tried to yell to one of the surfers. It was useless. "Dad!" I yelled again. I turned for the lifeguards up high on their platforms. I waved my arms in a crisscross over my head to get their attention.

"Hey!" I yelled. "Hey!" One was holding up the binoculars, but he was facing the other way.

So I started swimming toward my father. If I could get close enough, I could remind him just to tread water and rest, or I could get a board from someone for him to hold on to. I was a good swimmer. We all were. But I couldn't swim fast enough. I saw my father's head go under and then pop back up, and he was spluttering. Why wasn't he staying calm, like he'd told us to do? Why wasn't he realizing he was in a riptide?

"Dad!" I yelled. "Dad!" I stopped to rest and waved my arms in a crisscross again for the surfers, for the lifeguards. For anybody who would notice. Nobody did. I scanned the horizon for my mother on the raft, but I couldn't even see where she was. I looked back at my dad. He was still trying to swim straight in. "Stop!" I yelled. He went under again, and I was furious. How could he be so stupid?

I swam as hard as I could. "Hey," I breathed, kicking my way to the first surfer who might hear me. "Hey! Help!" I pulled at his leg the second I was close enough.

"What?" He was a teenager, and he looked annoyed.

I pointed to my father, who was going under again. "He needs help," I said. "He needs your board."

My father was flipping his head up and out of the water. His eyes were wide, mouth round, and you could see how hard it was for him to lift his arms.

"Hurry!" I yelled to the teenager.

He did. He paddled fast.

By the time I caught up, my father was clinging to the board, just outside of the rip.

"You scared me, dude," the surfer was saying.

My dad was breathing really heavy. The vein in his forehead was pulsing.

"Got a little rip going there, man," the surfer went. "Listen, when you get in those, you want to relax, you know?"

My father gulped in air and wiped his mouth. He didn't

even notice me there, treading water behind him. He didn't notice me following as the surfer paddled and then pointed his board straight in to shore while my dad hung on. I was right behind them.

"I'm okay," my dad breathed. "Thanks."

"You sure?" the teenager asked. "You seem kind of tired." My father nodded and let go of the board. He started swimming. I swam after him. He was going slow. His arms looked heavy. We passed my brother.

"What's going on?" Jack asked me.

"Dad almost drowned."

Jack followed me following my father. I watched my dad climb onto the beach, his dripping body bent, drooped. On the sand he wobbled, like he was drunk, and he kept wobbling all the way back to our blanket and umbrellas. Jack and I followed.

"What happened?" my mom asked. She must have swum in without anybody noticing her.

My father flapped his hand back toward the water and didn't answer. He was still breathing really heavy.

"You look ill," my mom went. "What happened?"

"He almost drowned," Jack told her.

"I did not almost drown." My father sank down hard onto his chair, making a smacking sound, and rubbed a towel over his head and face.

"Yes, you did," I insisted. Why was he lying?

"I'm fine," my father told me.

"I saw you." I remembered his face. The way it had kept going under. The way his eyes and mouth had been so round. I started to cry.

"Harvey?" my mom said. Jack was looking back and forth at my father and at me, all worried. I couldn't stop crying, and I was waiting for my dad to yell at me for it, which made me more mad and more scared.

"He did," I sobbed. "I saw it with my own eyes. He almost drowned."

My dad didn't yell. He pulled me to him and onto his wet lap.

"It's okay," he said, real gentle. "I'm all right."

"You're remembering Dad, right?" Jack asks me now.

"Yup," I say.

"Was he really drowning?"

"Yeah." I sit up and look out toward the brownish horizon. There's a ship way off in the distance. And a hang glider above us. "It was so weird, with all those people around." The hang glider is bright yellow and orange. It's peaceful to watch it.

"You saved his life," Jack tells me.

"Not according to him," I answer.

Now Jack sits up. "Isn't it interesting how you and I deal with what a pain in the ass he is?"

"What do you mean?"

"I get so into my music and movies. You know? I get so into it, he could be yelling or being a jerk right in the same room, and I'd barely hear him."

"Aren't you just that way naturally?" I ask.

"And you," Jack goes on, ignoring me and standing up on the trampoline. "You get so uptight you skim the surface of everything."

"What do you mean, I skim the surface?"

"You get nervous so quick you forget to stop and breathe."

"Breathe?" I snort. "That definitely came from Cameron." Then I smack my hand over my mouth. "I'm sorry," I say. "I'm sorry."

Jack starts jumping. "That's okay," he tells me. And half of his face smiles while the other half cries. "It did come from Cameron."

He jumps lightly, the bottoms of his feet just barely leaving the rubber on each ascent. Really it's more of a bounce.

"I'm not nervous," I say cautiously.

"Not nervous exactly." Jack bounces. His face readjusts back to normal. "Just . . . not relaxed."

"That's not true."

I stand up.

"It's not a criticism," Jack says. "It's a constructive observation."

He bounces for a while, facing me. The hang glider is circling over us. I'm thinking about a lot of different things all at once.

"Will you ever stop being sad?" I ask him. He doesn't stop bouncing, and his face flashes to that half-crying–half-smiling mask and then back to normal, and then he shoves some of the dark, damp hair out of his face.

"No," he says. "I don't see how."

Back on the beach Ellen says, "Sea-rene."

"What?" I squeeze my hair to get the water out and lie down on my towel.

Jack's spreading his at my feet.

"Everything looked so serene," Ellen says. "You guys out

there on the trampoline. That ship way off on the horizon. That hang glider. It was like watching a silent movie."

"Do you like silent movies?" Jack asks her.

"Jack says I'm superficial," I interrupt, "and I only skim the surface of things because of my father."

"She's not superficial exactly," Ellen tells Jack.

"Oh, thanks," I say.

"She's just scared."

"I know." Jack squirts sunblock onto his hand and starts to rub his arms and chest with it.

"I'm not scared," I say. They're pissing me off. I don't even know what they're talking about. Besides, Ellen is supposed to defend me. "I'm dumping you for the Ashleys," I tell her.

"That's what I mean." Now Jack's rubbing his legs.

"What?" I say.

"You're the only one who calls them the Ashleys," Jack tells me.

"That's not true." I look at Ellen through my sunglasses. "Everyone calls them the Ashleys."

Ellen rolls her eyes.

"What?" I say. "You call them that."

She shakes her head. "You came up with it."

"Maybe, but you use it."

"Actually," she says very carefully, "I don't."

I stop to think about it. I'm sure I've heard her say "the Ashleys" before. I'm sure of it. I watch Jack get rid of the excess sunblock by wiping the webs of every two fingers onto his chin.

"Do you know that Ashley Jasper has a little brother who's retarded?" Ellen asks me.

"Is that Ashley One or Ashley Two?"

"See?" Jack says to Ellen.

She won't look at me.

"I'm not superficial," I argue at them. They don't argue back. "I'm not scared, either," I say. "The Ashleys are bitchy snobs. What would I be scared of?"

"It's more complicated than that." Jack lies back on his towel.

"Like you know so much," I tell him.

"I just see more of the big picture," Jack says.

"So you're better than I am," I say.

"Could you guys stop it?" Ellen asks. Her voice is off. Raggedy somehow.

Jack and I both squint at her. She's staring up at that hang glider, biting her lip.

"Sorry," I mutter.

"It doesn't matter what you were scared of before," Ellen says. "You're scared now, and it's messing you up."

"I'm okay," I tell her.

"No, you're not." Ellen's still gazing at the sky. "My mother was right. Shell shock. I think she's right about all three of us. But especially about you."

"What do you mean?" I say. "You were in the car too. You got hurt way worse than I did. And you're tired constantly, even when it has nothing to do with your leg or your ribs, so don't even say that's it, and you space out and get bored all the time. And Jack." I look at him, lying on his back with his eyes closed. "Jack's going to be sad for the rest of his life."

Ellen answers in this really gentle voice that's not like her at all. "Jack and I can sleep, and—"

"You sleep too much," I interrupt.

She waits for more than a second before she speaks again, and when she does, her voice stays soft, careful. "And we can drive. Well, I'll be able to as soon as my leg heals. Plus, we can concentrate usually."

"It's all of us," I argue. "It's bad for all of us. Jack cries all the time. I see him." He doesn't move. On his back, with his eyes closed, tanned skin glistening in the sun, anybody who didn't know would think he was dozing. "I see you," I tell him. He starts to hum.

"What are you humming?" Ellen asks him.

"Guid Merge."

"I see you crying sometimes, Jack, when you don't think anybody is looking or can tell. And I hear you in your room at home. I heard you two nights in a row last week." He keeps humming, eyes closed.

"We don't shake," Ellen tells me quietly. "We don't have fake heart attacks every second and nightmares."

"I have nightmares," Jack says. No more humming.

"Okay," Ellen agrees. "So do I. But we don't wake up screaming and freaked out. We wake up sad."

"I'm sad," I say, and it sounds ridiculous.

"I know, Anna," Ellen says as nicely as she's ever said anything to me. "But also you're really messed up."

16

THREE HOURS AFTER I GET HOME, SETH IS ON OUR DOORSTEP.

"Anna!" Jack yells, even though I'm right there behind him.

"Hi," I say to Seth.

Jack steps aside.

"Hi," Seth says to me. "I like your shades." He holds out his hand, palm up. M&M's.

I don't take any. My brother takes a few. "Are you going to invite him in?" Jack asks.

"Would you like to leave now?" I ask Jack back.

"Delighted," Jack goes, and he nods his head at Seth and disappears up the stairs.

"Okay," I tell Seth. "Come in."

I lead him to the family room and plop myself down on the L of the couch. I keep my sunglasses on, even though I don't need them indoors.

He stays standing. "Anna, I'm sorry I was such an idiot that night."

"It doesn't matter," I go, even though it does matter.

He sits down, but as far away as possible. "I'd been wanting to say a lot of stuff to you about the accident for a long time," Seth goes. "But . . . it's . . . you know . . . I guess the way it came out was . . . well, stupid."

"The truth is," I tell him, "we don't even really know each other."

"We were starting to," Seth says. "All of us, I mean. Jason and Lisa and Ellen."

"Who did you used to hang out with?" I ask Seth.

He digs into his pocket and then feeds some M&M's into his mouth. "Leo Feld and Rimi and Justin and that crowd," Seth says, crunching. "We still hang out sometimes."

"Ellen and my brother tell me I'm all messed up," I say. "I don't think I'm such great girlfriend material right now."

"Maybe that's just a way of saying you're not into me," Seth goes.

"Maybe."

He looks bummed, and then he starts to smile a little. "You're sort of a bitch," he tells me.

"Screw you," I tell him back.

"Okay," he goes, and he scoots over next to me. Then he lifts the sunglasses off my face and holds my cheeks in his hands. He doesn't kiss me. We just look at each other for a while.

"You got tan," he goes.

It's hard not to smile. His hands are big and warm.

"And your hair is the color of fire now."

He has pretty eyes. Brown with black rings around the outside.

"You've got a cat's eye," he tells me. He pulls his head back and squints. "Your pupil is vertical."

"I know," I say. "It might never get round again."

"Supreme." He smiles.

He doesn't let go of my face. My heart starts to beat fast. "My brother told me no girl can resist this move," he says finally, his face inches away from mine.

I knock his hands away. "Your brother doesn't know anything," I lie. But I keep hold of one of his index fingers, between us.

"So, what's going on?" I ask. He pulls a curl with his free hand. Then he pulls another one. I shake him off. "What's all this stuff you've wanted to say to me since the accident?"

"I really, really love your curls."

"I'm serious," I tell him. "What did you want to say?"

He sits up straight and scoots back a little. Shoves his free hand into his pocket and pulls out two M&M's. A green and an orange. "I just . . . um . . ." He slips the M&M's back into his pocket, and we listen to them click against each other. "I just feel . . . bad for you. Really, really bad."

"Oh," I say.

My uncle Buck is a gourmet cook. My aunt Jerry takes in foster dogs. Besides a Great Dane named Mamie they've had forever, there's always a few greyhounds and a mutt or two.

We hear barking even before we're out of the car.

"Welcome to the zoo," my father mumbles. Which is what he says every year. My mom and I carry two pumpkin pies and a bowl of stuffing, but still the dogs jump all over my father. Dogs love him for some reason.

"Off, Cyrus!" Aunt Jerry yells. "Off, Nixon! Off, Lucifer! Off! Off!"

"Lucifer?" Jack asks her. Aunt Jerry grabs me and Jack at the same time. She's the only one so far not too careful about my eye.

"I'm sorry, you guys," she whispers to us. "I'm so, so sorry."

"Get away!" my dad's yelling at the dogs. "Get away!"

"You have to say 'off,' Dad," Jack tells him, pulling free of Aunt Jerry, his face that half-and-half mask.

Mamie is too old to be a jumper. She lies right in the doorway between the kitchen and dining room, so you sort of have to leap over her. She's almost the size of a small pony.

"God damn it," my dad mutters when he spills some of his beer, stumbling over her. Mamie licks it up and then goes for his hand. He spills more beer trying to avoid her big head.

We sit down to eat almost right away. The table is covered with soups and salads and pumpkin breads and cranberry dishes and sweet-potato purees and two bowls of rice with flower petals garnishing the tops. We'll never finish it all, and Aunt Jerry will take the leftover main courses and half the fresh desserts to a soup kitchen later tonight. She'll make Jack and me come with her. She does that every year.

"There won't be any lawsuits?" Uncle Buck asks while he carves the turkey.

"No," my father says, shoving Nixon's head out of his crotch. I hadn't even thought about that.

"It wasn't Anna's fault," my mother says. "It wasn't anybody's fault. It was an accident."

"Not even a civil suit?" Uncle Buck asks. He puts the dark meat on one platter and the white meat on another. I pick up two big serving forks, waiting to add them when my uncle is done carving.

"No, Buck," my mother says. She sounds mad. "There won't be any lawsuits."

"Lucky," Buck says. "That's lucky."

"Stop that, Anna," my father tells me.

"Stop what?" I ask him. Everybody looks at me. I don't get it at first. Then I notice: The two forks are clacking together in my hand, making a fast, metallic rhythm, like a pair of castanets. I drop them onto the table and shove both hands in my lap. "Sorry," I say.

I'm refilling the water pitchers in the kitchen halfway through the meal. Aunt Jerry and my mother are pulling more bread out of the oven. It's infused with some sort of garlic pumpkin flavor, and Uncle Buck won't allow us to eat any that's not warm.

"It's called EMDR," Aunt Jerry's saying. "It's a kind of therapy for trauma survivors. I really think you should try it for her."

"For me?" I ask. "Are you talking about me?" Am I a trauma survivor?

"Get away!" I hear my father yelling.

"Off, Lucifer!" Uncle Buck and Jack yell right after that. If I hadn't just been called a trauma survivor, I'd laugh.

"Dad doesn't want me in therapy," I tell them.

"Your father is clueless," Aunt Jerry says, annoyed.

"Jerry," my mom goes. "You don't have to—"

"Just look at her," Aunt Jerry tells my mother. "Look at her!"

My mother looks at me. Aunt Jerry looks at me. I wonder if this is how the dogs feel when Jerry goes to pick one out.

What do they see?

Lucifer comes with us in the car. Everybody else stays home. Uncle Buck will get the desserts ready—the ones we haven't taken along with the leftovers—while my parents moan about how sick they feel from eating so much.

"So, how have you been really?" Aunt Jerry asks Jack.

He shakes his head. "I don't know. You should ask how Anna's been."

"It's obvious how Anna is," Jerry says. "You. You're less obvious."

"He's sad," I say.

"Shut up," he tells me, but not mean.

Lucifer is a mutt. He's small and energetic. He keeps trying to lick our faces. He wiggles from the front to the backseat, back and forth, first to me, then to Jack, then to me. If I'd been prepared for Lucifer, I'd have dug up my eye shield.

"And how have the two of you been together?" Jerry asks. She's my mom's older sister, but she's different from my mother. She gets right to the point. She doesn't let things go. She reminds me a little bit of Ellen's mom, actually, only not so stylish. To be honest, with her short hair and boxy body and something about her skin, she sort of looks like a man.

"What do you mean?" I ask.

"I think you know what I mean," she says. I glance at Jack. He's staring out the window.

"You mean that I killed his girlfriend," I tell Aunt Jerry.

"Shut up," Jack tells the window.

"That's not exactly what I mean," she goes. "And that's not exactly the truth of it either." She glances at me in her rearview.

Lucifer leaps from Jack's lap back to mine.

"Let me tell you what I wish for you," Jerry says after Jack and I stay quiet. She pulls into the Salvation Army parking lot. "I wish that when you're the ages of your mom and me, you see each other more than Thanksgiving and Christmas each year. I hope that you talk to each other a lot, about real things, the things that matter, and that you're involved in the lives of each other's children." It's embarrassing. How serious she's being. How . . . I don't know. Earnest.

Lucifer's on her lap now, snuggling in, even though we're all about to get out of the car. Jack glances back at me. His face is red.

"Siblings should be friends," Aunt Jerry says. "The two of you, especially, should be friends." Why us especially?

"Okay," Jack says.

"Okay," I say. I think we both just want her to stop.

"You didn't kill Cameron," Jack tells me suddenly, twisting all the way around from the front seat to see me.

"Yes, I did," I tell him back.

"No, you didn't," he says.

"Yes, I did."

"Stop it," Aunt Jerry says. "We have to bring the food in."

So we stop.

· · ·

Back at the house, in front of the dessert spread, with steaming cups of coffee and cappuccino and exotic teas, Uncle Buck doesn't let us dig in until we say what we're thankful for. We do it that way every year. Nothing before the main meal. No prayers or toasts or anything. Thanks always come just before dessert. It's mandatory. Uncle Buck tells my dad to begin. My father puts his palms on the table and looks around at all of us.

"Get away!" he yells when Lucifer tries to climb on his lap.

"Off!" Uncle Buck pulls Lucifer back by the collar. My dad takes a deep breath. The vein in his forehead starts pulsing.

"Well," he says. "We have a lot to be thankful for this . . . ," and then he stops talking. He looks at me and Jack, and he tries to say something, only instead his face crunches inward and goes pink. He turns to my mother and makes a snorting sound, and then he looks at me and Jack again, and he shakes his head, and he stares at the middle of the table, and he goes, in this awful, high-pitched voice, "I can't." And he just sits there, shaking and then crying, while we watch, frozen, and Mamie lurches to her feet from the foot of his chair and whines and starts to lick his face, and Uncle Buck yanks her away, and it's almost as bad as the screaming, stopped.

17

"YOU HAVE SOMETHING CALLED POST-TRAUMATIC STRESS DISORDER,"
the therapist tells me. Her name is Frances. She's about my
mom's age, and she's got a lot of freckles, which are sort of
cute and funny-looking at the same time.

"Nightmares, startle response, panic attacks, inability to
concentrate, avoidance behaviors."

"Avoidance, like avoiding driving?"

She nods. "Those can all be symptoms of PTSD."

"Did you buy that at Cinnamon Toast?" I ask her. She looks
down at her flowing clothes in muted colors.

"Uh . . . ," she goes.

"My best friend's mom owns that store," I say. "Ellen. The
one who was in the car with me."

"Oh," Frances says.

It's the third time I've seen Frances in two weeks. My parents have seen her once, together.

"How come Ellen doesn't have post-traumatic stress whatever?"

"Disorder," Frances reminds me. "PTSD. She might have it. But I don't know Ellen, so I couldn't say."

It's not that I don't like Frances. She's okay. It's that I'm embarrassed about being in therapy.

"It means I'm crazy, right?" I say. "Jack and Ellen think so. They think I'm completely and totally insane."

"Do you think you're insane?" Frances asks.

"I don't think most sixteen-year-olds go around feeling like they're going to die from heart attacks every time they get near a steering wheel," I say. Not to mention shaking practically all the time and nightmares every single night.

"Actually," Frances tells me, "in your case that's a normal reaction to an abnormal life experience."

"If it's so normal, why isn't Ellen having the same reaction as I am?"

"First of all, she wasn't driving. But also, Ellen was drunk and then passed out," Frances says. "Her brain was having an entirely different experience from yours."

"We were in the same car," I say. "We were in the same accident."

"Were you?" Frances asks.

Now I'm thinking she's the insane one. If I were a little younger, I'd probably look at her and go, "Duh." But I just stay quiet.

"Anna. There's nothing crazy about you. Listen." She leans

forward, and her freckles slightly change color somehow. They get darker. "When a trauma occurs, it seems to get locked in the nervous system with the original pictures, sounds, and feelings. A part of the brain that's involved in handling thought and language shuts down. Another part of the brain that knows only body sensations and emotions gets lit up. Way up. If those two parts of the brain don't find a way to reconnect, we can end up with symptoms like the ones you have."

She stops talking and leans back in her black leather chair. I'm sitting at the corner of her couch. It's red and has these small, cream-colored suede throw pillows, which are really, really smooth. I can't stop stroking them, as if they're little pets or something.

"Well, how do I get the two parts of my brain to reconnect, so I'm not such a head case?" I ask.

"There are different ways to treat PTSD," Frances tells me, "including taking medication for the anxiety and panic-attack part. There's also something called exposure therapy, which would involve getting you behind the wheel of a car before you really want to, and then making you drive. Then there're ways of making use of body sensations. We'll use elements of that today. And there's something called EMDR, which is my vote on what's most likely to get your brain reconnected."

"I don't want to drive." It's the only part of what she's just said that I hear. *Getting you behind the wheel of a car again.* I feel my heart chipping away at the inside of my chest, just at the thought.

"All right," Frances says. "We won't do that, then."

My heart's still pounding, though.

"What's going on?" she asks.

"What do you mean?"

"Your face is red, and you're sweating."

I wipe the tops of my thumbs down my temples, which are hot and damp.

"That's your body's response to the memory of the accident," Frances says. "You were thinking about having to drive, right?"

I nod.

"See how you're physically reacting to that thought?"

"I guess," I say.

"What kind of feelings are you having, thinking about it?" she asks.

"Shaking. Sweating. Hot," I say. "Kind of like I could throw up."

"Okay. Those are body sensations. What kind of emotional feelings are you having?" she asks.

"Scared. Embarrassed. Nervous," I say. I am crazy. I must be.

"Put your feet flat on the floor." Frances sits up straight, uncrosses her legs, and does it herself. "Like this. Really feel the bottoms of your feet supported by the rug and the wood beneath."

I untangle myself and copy her. I slide my butt to the edge of the couch and flatten both my feet inside my black leather boots with the zippers up the sides.

"Press down a little bit and see if you can feel the ground pressing back, solid under the soles of your feet."

"Okay," I say after a second. I'm a little calmed down, I think.

"Now take a couple of deep breaths," Frances tells me. "Like this." She breathes in really, really slow through her nose. She holds it a second and then blows the air out through her mouth, long and deep. It's a little weird. It looks like Ellen's mom, sort of, on her yoga mat.

But I do it anyway. I take a breath.

"Slower," Frances tells me. "Go slower." So I do. "How does your body feel now?" she asks after I blow the air out.

"I thought therapy was about talking," I say. "Not breathing. Or . . . you know . . . feet."

"This is uncomfortable for you," she tells me.

"Kind of." But as weird as it is, having my feet solidly on the floor and breathing deep like that does make me feel better. "I guess I'm not feeling as embarrassed," I admit to Frances.

"Good," she goes. "So you get a sense of how your body can cue emotions, and how emotions can cue your body. Right?"

I nod.

"So if you notice you're feeling anxious or afraid, you can use this to help soothe yourself. Just put your feet flat on the ground and breathe."

"Uh-huh," I say. "But . . ." I stroke the cream-colored pillow, worrying that the nightmares are too big and the shaking is too strong to be fixed so fast by some new way of sitting and breathing.

"What is it?" Frances asks.

I stop stroking and look at all the certificates on her wall. There're a bunch of them, and the one on the left middle row is crooked. "Am I going to be okay?" I think about how mad my dad is at how messed up I am now, and I feel that thick ink in my chest. "I mean, really okay?"

"Yes, Anna." I can feel her staring at me, and I pull my eyes from her certificates on the wall to look back at her. Her freckled face is so confident. "You're going to be fine." The ink thins out a lot. Not all the way. But a lot. It's a relief. To hear that from someone who maybe actually knows.

Rob's SUV is the easiest car for Ellen, with her wheelchair, compared with Ellen's mom's Volvo or our new Honda. So instead of going to school separately, Jack and I and Ellen and Rob start showing up together.

"How new is your car?" Ellen asks Rob as Jack helps her into the wheelchair. I'm holding her book bag, and Rob's kicking at the back left tire, worrying it's got a leak. He doesn't say anything. "Because it smells new," Ellen goes. "And it's spotless."

"Rob's a clean freak," Jack says. The air has that December edge to it that turns our breath into mini steam clouds.

"So when did you get the car?" Ellen asks again.

Rob holds out two fingers. We're heading out of the parking lot and toward the school building.

"Two months ago?" she guesses. Rob smiles.

"Two years," Jack corrects.

"No way," I say. I spot Lisa exiting the front door of school and walking down the steps onto the lawn toward us.

"Yep," Jack goes.

Lisa meets us near the flagpole. "They've got prom planning committee posted."

I don't know why she's telling us. We're not planning-committee people. To tell you the truth, we're not prom people either.

"I thought we didn't find out until tomorrow," Ellen says. Before I can even register that one, Lisa's talking again.

"Jack's on music, and so is Ellen."

What? We're walking up the outside double stairs now, and I'm shoving past kids harder than I usually do. Rob and Jack carry Ellen, in her chair, as if she doesn't weigh a thing. They're supposed to wheel her in to the side door, where there's a ramp, but we never bother.

"Rob, you're on theme and decoration."

"Excellent," he says.

"Wow," Lisa goes. "You have a really deep voice."

"You guys signed up to be on prom?" I ask.

We're inside. The bell is going to ring any second, and I just want the day to be over already.

"Not me," Lisa says. "I just passed the posting by accident."

"Hi," Jason goes, joining us.

"I wanted decent music this year," Ellen says. "I told you."

"No, you didn't."

"Take your sin-glasses off." She's supposed to remind me when I forget indoors, which is a lot of the time. Jason's looking back and forth at her and me, trying to figure out what's going on.

She went last year with this senior, Alan Frendleman. They broke up five days later because he decided he was too old to have a tenth-grade girlfriend. Ellen didn't really like him anyway. I mean, she liked him as a friend, but she said he was a bad kisser and worse at other things. Whatever.

"I didn't know you signed up," Ellen's saying to Jack. Then she turns to Jason. "Did you?"

"For prom?" Jason asks.

"Who do you think you're even going with?" I say to Ellen, but Rob's bass voice drowns out mine.

"He did it for Cameron," he rumbles.

We look at him. He looks at Jack.

"She was into it," Jack explains. "She convinced me."

"Duh," Lisa goes. "She would have been voted prom queen."

"Actually," Jack says, "she was going to . . ."

We all stop, as if there's a red light or some sort of signal. We just stop right where we are, in the center of the T intersection of the science rooms and math hall. We stand still and stare at Jack. He stares back, and his face fights itself.

"Anyway," he mutters. He shakes his head at Rob. "Come on." They take off.

Lisa starts walking after a second. Then she stops. Then she starts and keeps going. Ellen and Jason and I stay where we are, watching Lisa's back.

"I even e-mailed Anna about it," Ellen tells Jason. He arches his eyebrow. I see Seth moving toward us from the end of the hall.

"No, she didn't," I say to Jason. "She never said a word."

They start meeting for their stupid committees in, like, February or something. It's stupid. We've always said how stupid it is.

"I did," Ellen argues. "I'm sure of it."

The bell rings. Seth walks up and pulls a curl and kisses my cheek.

I push him off and spin away and don't even wait to see how they're going to get Ellen up the stairs for French IV.

18

SETH FINDS ME DURING LUNCH. I'M HIDING IN THE GIRLS' ROOM at the back of the back gym lockers. It's a bathroom Ellen and I never use because it's always filled with smoke and there're only two stalls and Marcy Cunningham gives blow jobs in here all the time. Seth marches straight through the door.

"Guy!" some girl waiting yells.

"Come on," he says to me.

"You're going to get into trouble," I say back.

"Life without parole," he goes. "Now, come on."

"Get out!" this girl yells.

Marcy Cunningham walks in. "Get out," she tells everybody.

"Come on," Seth says. I walk out with him.

"So, what's the matter?" He steers me away from the lunch-room and toward the side exit. There's a brick wall out there, and in the spring all these purple and white flowers sprout up along the face of it. But it's not spring, and when we get to the wall, it's not pretty. It's just brick. "What's the matter?" he asks again.

"Everything," I say. I lean my butt on the low edge. It's cold and sharp.

"Oh," Seth goes. He stands in front of me and starts pulling my curls and letting them bounce back. There's nobody else out here. I let him pull.

"Where are your shades?" he asks. I must have dropped them in the bathroom. It makes me realize my right eye isn't freaking out in the daylight.

"I guess I don't need them anymore," I say.

He keeps pulling. He goes, "Boing, boing," under his breath.

"What's your next big thing?" I ask him. "You never told me. From that day at Ellen's. You know. Charisma. Heart attack."

"Oh, yeah," he says. "Send a dollar."

"What?"

"Send a dollar. I started it already. I put an ad in the *City Trib* classified section. It just says, 'Send a dollar.' With a post office box address. That day at Ellen's I was working on the wording."

"I don't get it," I say.

"I want to see how many people actually send money."

"You're kidding me."

"Nope."

"You have a post office box address?"

"I do now."

"Isn't that expensive?"

"I have a feeling dollars will be arriving shortly to cover the cost."

"Isn't that illegal? Can you just take people's money like that? Doesn't there have to be a cause or something? I mean, you could get into trouble."

"Life without par . . . ," he starts, but he doesn't finish.

"Stop making me feel stupid."

"I'm not making you feel anything." But he is.

"I don't want to like you," I tell him.

"Yeah, you're kind of strange about that."

"I don't know why." It's embarrassing for some reason.

"Me neither," he says. "I'm a good catch."

I take his hands and put one on each of my cheeks. It feels nice. Safe.

"Don't kiss me," I tell him.

"Okay," he says. "Can I kiss you this afternoon, though?" His face is almost touching mine. I can smell his breath. Chocolate and peanut butter.

"No," I say. "I have therapy."

"You can't kiss on the same days as therapy?" he asks. "Is that a law?"

"Yes."

"Oh," he says.

Ellen passes me a note in biology. If Ms. Riffing catches cell phones in use, she confiscates them and then uses them to call parents to tell them how great their kids are. She calls them every day from the kid's cell, and at about day four she'll mention that she'll be keeping the kid's phone until the end of the marking period.

Why are you so mad? Ellen's handwriting slants to the right, and her letters are tall and angled. Not curvy and round like Lisa's.

You never told me, I pass back. *After Christmas you and Jack are going to be hanging out together while I'm doing nothing.*

I did tell you. And I didn't even know about Jack.

Fine, I write. *Forget it.*

You'll get to have more alone time with Seth, anyway.

Big deal, I write back.

Stop moping, she writes. *It's just a stupid prom committee. It's just a stupid prom.*

Exactly! And I draw a frown face.

Oh, come on. She draws a smiley face.

I think about Cameron and know I'm a complete spoiled bitch brat, because I'm alive at least, and I suck up how bad I'm feeling straight to somewhere in the bottom of my stomach.

I'm not moping, I write back. *M. C. was in the science hall bathroom again.*

Which guy?

Didn't see.

I feel sorry for her, Ellen writes.

So do I. So, Jason's not on any prom committees?

I wish. He is so amazing.

He's gay, I remind her.

But he hasn't had a boyfriend since I've known him.

He's not straight, Ellen. He's picky. He's got class.

I know. Okay. What are you doing after school?

Therapy, I write. *You?*

Doctor. I get my short cast soon.

It's been almost two months. I can't believe it.

I know, she scribbles.

SATs are almost here.

I know.

Christmas is almost here.

I know. She draws a face with a half smile, half frown. It reminds me of Jack.

I feel like shit.

Yeah, she writes, and I'm reading it, and then Ms. Riffing is standing over me. She whirls around and around, saying something about the path of mitochondria. Actually, I think she's being a mitochondrion. Everyone is laughing. Ms. Riffing doesn't stop talking or whirling. Just holds out her hand. I have to pass over the note in time with her spin.

She uses the note to be some part of a cell, or maybe an enzyme—I'm not really sure—and then she crumples it up and stuffs it in her mouth and keeps swirling, and Ellen and I pay attention after that.

Frances is trying to explain EMDR.

"Bilateral stimulation of the brain used in a certain way," she's telling me, "seems to unlock the nervous system and to help people with PTSD."

"Wait," I say, holding up a little rectangular box that looks sort of like a gray iPod. "Is this the bilateral stimulation?" It has headphones attached to it and also another set of wires that end in two matching plastic handles, each about the size of a mussel. They vibrate in your hands, one at a time, back and forth, when the little box is turned on. The headphones make this soft snapping sound, one ear at a time.

"Yep," Frances says. "I also use left-right eye movements with a lot of people, but since you've had an eye injury, we won't do it that way with you."

I put down the box, with its headphones and hand buzzers and pick up a suede pillow. "Hearing clicks back and forth and getting my hands buzzed back and forth is going to unlock my nervous system?"

She nods.

"I still don't get how."

"We think it works a little bit like what happens when we're in deep sleep," Frances explains. "We all need a minimum amount of sleep in order not to get too crazy. Right?"

"If you say so," I go.

"Okay," she says. "You know how in deep sleep your eyes move back and forth very quickly?"

"I guess," I say, stroking the pillow.

"It may be that those eye movements are a kind of bilateral stimulation that helps people process daily experiences," Frances says. "That way our brains don't get overloaded from all the stimuli we take in each day."

"So deep sleep is like mini EMDR for everybody?" I ask.

"Theoretically."

I put down the pillow and pick up the gray box again. I take a buzzer in each hand and turn it on. *Buzz. Buzz.* And I thought deep breathing was weird. I turn it off.

"Today we're not even going to work on the accident," she tells me.

"Why not?"

"First we need a safe place," she says, "and then we need

some inner resources for you to call on if you ever need them."

"A safe place?" I ask. "Do my parents know we're doing this?"

Frances smiles. "I explained EMDR to them." She has perfectly even teeth, except for this one that's longer than the others and pointy. A fang. "Why do you ask?"

"No offense," I tell her. "But I have a feeling they'd think this is . . . um . . . like, a waste of time."

"Listen," Frances goes. "If you don't stop having nightmares and the shakes and panic attacks after four more sessions, we'll try something else."

"Like forcing me to drive?" I ask.

"No," she says. "Maybe medication."

"But I don't want medication, either," I say.

"Okay," Frances agrees. "So how about trying something weird instead?"

It's hard to fall asleep because I know I'm going to have one of those nightmares, and they scare me, plus they wake everyone up, and it's embarrassing, even though when my mother comes in, she just stays quiet and strokes my sweaty head. So tonight I try to use what we did in therapy the way Frances suggested.

She had me imagine a place that felt totally safe and comfortable. She made me describe the whole thing to her. Every now and then she'd turn those hand buzzers on—I didn't like the headphones—and they'd vibrate back and forth. It's a pink sand beach I made up. Not Commons End, with its greenish, choppy water. Another place. A Caribbean sea, magical, with dazzling turquoise waves that are steady and even, rolling in from the horizon in a predictable, slow rhythm. Between each wave the water's as still as glass. You can hear seagulls and the lapping of wavelets and the breeze rustling through palm trees. It smells like coconut sunblock and seaweed, and it's warm without being too hot. So now I try to think of that. It sort of helps, but still. It's not like I'm actually in this place. It's not like it can actually keep me from having a nightmare. That much I know.

I think of the other two things we did. Frances calls them inner resources. More weirdness. First she had me create a protector figure. She said it could be real, imagined, dead, or alive. I had to think about the qualities I'd want a protector to have: strong, fast, loving, smart, levelheaded, magical. I picked a dolphin. A big gray dolphin with a white underbelly. So I make myself see him now at the magical Caribbean beach with the dazzling turquoise waves, and I swim with him and feel my body relaxing, but then the minute I know I might really fall asleep, I'm wide awake again.

So I picture my adviser. This one has to be wise and smart and levelheaded and able to see problems and solutions from all angles. I've picked an old woman. She's sort of tall and thin, but not in a scrawny way. More regal, like a queen or something, and she has white hair tied back in a fancy knot, and she's dressed in flowing clothes, and she's got wrinkled skin and this kind, knowing expression. So now I put her on the beach. She sits on a three-legged wooden stool in the shade and watches me play in the blue, blue water with the dolphin.

• • •

"Anna!"

My father's sitting on my bed. He hasn't turned the light on, but still I can see that he's got a cup of water in his hands.

"I'm sorry," I tell him. "I didn't mean to wake everybody up again."

A bloody glass wave looming over me and Jack, and screaming shattering out of the wave, and blood splattering our faces, looming and red and wet and huge, and screaming, screaming, screaming.

"Drink," my dad goes, so I take the glass and drink.

A bloody glass wave with my father standing behind it, about to throw another one, and my brother with his hands up and out, and screaming and screaming and screaming.

"I'm going to throw up," I say, and he moves fast to grab my wastebasket and hold it near my face, but I don't throw up after all. "Okay," I say after a minute. "Maybe I'm not." I'm shaking. "Thanks," I say. "Sorry."

"I hate to see you like this," he tells me, putting the wastebasket on the floor and sitting down on the edge of the bed.

"I'm okay," I tell him.

"I wanted you on medication," my father goes. "But your therapist said to give her six sessions first with this EMDR thing."

"I don't want to take medicine."

"You need to be able to drive."

"I know," I say. "I'm sorry."

"You need to stop having these nightmares."

"Yeah," I go. "I know. I'm sorry."

"I want you to put this thing behind you."

"Dad, I'm really sorry."

"Stop saying you're sorry, Anna," he orders.

"Sorr . . . ," I go.

"Here," he says. "Sit up a minute." He straightens and smoothes my sheets and then plumps my pillow, just like Ellen might do it. "Now, lie back." I obey. "Try to get some sleep."

"Dad," I say as he's leaving my room. He turns around, but it's too dark to see his face all that well. "Are you going to get therapy?"

"No," he goes. "Why?"

I'm thinking about Thanksgiving. About his voice, so high pitched and awful. About him crying.

"I don't know."

"Get some sleep, Anna."

"You're not in such great shape either," I tell him through the dark. He pauses, just outside my door. I'm frozen, waiting for him to turn around again and yell at me. But he doesn't. I hear him just standing there for a really long time before he finally moves away and down the hall.

19

IT'S OUR LAST STUDY SESSION BEFORE THE SAT.

"Three hundred and thirty-four?" Jason's asking. We're at Ellen's, as usual. She and I made chocolate-chip cookies before everybody came over. Actually, I made them while Ellen sat in her wheelchair, leg propped up, and drank peppermint schnapps straight out of her parents' liquor cabinet. While I was scraping the last cookies off the sheet and onto a plate, Ellen poured water from my glass into the schnapps bottle to hide her crime.

"Three hundred and thirty-six," Seth goes, chewing his ninth cookie.

"What are you going to do with the money?" Lisa asks.

"I think it's unethical," Ellen says. She opens up her study guide. "It's taking advantage of stupid people." She looks down at the book. "Ugh," she goes. "I'm going to be so glad when this is over."

"How do you know they're stupid?" Seth asks. "Maybe they're just generous."

"Right," Ellen goes.

"Or bored," Jason suggests.

"Whatever," Ellen says. "Come on. We've done practically no math."

"We spent all last week on math," Jason says.

"Well, it's not enough. We stink at it," Ellen complains.

"I'm going to buy you a good mood," Seth goes.

"What?"

"With the money from all the stupid people," Seth tells her. "I'm going to buy you a good mood."

"I like that idea," Jason goes.

"I'm never hanging with you again," Ellen tells him.

"I like Seth's idea too," I say.

Ellen glares at us. "You people suck."

When I get home, Jack's in the kitchen, working on his laptop. He's got a not-too-bad song on low volume.

"Another review?" I ask him.

He stabs at a key and scans the screen. "No," he goes. "Amen Calling."

"What?"

"Amen Calling," he repeats.

We look at each other for a confused second before I get it. "Oh," I go. "Don't tell me Another Review is the name of a band?"

He gets it too. He laughs and turns off Amen Calling. "Yeah," he says. "It is. I was surprised you'd heard of it."

"Anyway," I go.

He nods at the computer screen. "Postings for Cameron," he explains.

My face gets hot. I remember what Frances told me, and I try to think about what my hot face is letting me know. What my body's telling me. It's not hard: My face is flushed because I feel embarrassed and ashamed because I still haven't looked at Cameron's memorial Web site. Much less written anything for it.

Jack looks up. "You want to see?" He turns the laptop a little toward me.

I shake my head. "I've got to study."

He slides the laptop back where it was. "You'll get to take them again," he says.

"Yeah," I go. "But still." He got 1490 on his. I'll never get that. Never.

"Cameron didn't do so great on them," Jack tells me.

"Really?" I ask. "What's not so great?" I'm thinking for Cameron that probably means at least 1400.

"She had trouble breaking a thousand," Jack goes.

"No way," I say.

"Yeah." He nods. "She did really bad on standardized tests."

I'm not sure what to do. We haven't talked about her at all, and the last time I tried, he lost it. So I stand here.

"She wasn't going to college right off the bat anyway," Jack tells me.

"Really?" I figure it's safest if I don't say too much.

"She was thinking of taking a year off to work."

"But she was so smart," I say. "Even with bad SATs she could have gone anywhere, right?"

"She thought it would be cool to just . . . you know . . . live for a year."

The minute he says it, it's like the room shrinks. Just gets small and cramped. *Live.* It's weird how things come out of our mouths that we don't plan. I look at Jack's mask of a face, and I don't know what to do. He drops his head straight down on the table, next to the laptop. *Live.* His forehead makes a thunking sound when it hits.

"Go away," Jack says. His voice is muffled.

"Jack," I say.

"Leave," he goes.

The first time Jack threw me out was the summer of the sharks. We weren't so young anymore. Eleven and twelve maybe. Twelve and thirteen. I'm not sure.

My father was frowning at the newspaper. "This isn't good."

We were sitting around the table, in front of the glass wall with a view of green skylighted roofs tapering to the gray slate sparkle of the ocean farther in the distance.

"What?" my mom asked. She'd made waffles for us. We always got special breakfasts at the beach. When we were really little, it was the assortment pack of mini cereals. The sweetened kind you can open and pour milk right into the box. Other times my mom made us chocolate-chip pancakes. That day it was peach-and-powdered-sugar waffles.

"Sharks," my dad said.

"Sharks?"

"Apparently small blue sharks have been swimming in shallow waters close to shore." My father was half reading, half telling. "A girl had her calf bitten."

"No," my mom said. She sifted some powdered sugar onto her half-eaten waffle.

"Yes."

"Around here?" I speared my next bite with my fork. "Really?"

"Not so far," my father said. "Near Ocracoke two swimmers were bitten on their lower legs just before sundown." He held out his plate for my mom to serve him another helping.

"Can we still swim?" I asked.

"Don't talk with your mouth full," my father answered. "You're going to choke."

I chewed madly.

"The lifeguards are the experts," my mother said. "They won't let us in the water if it's not safe. We'll read the board."

"They should have flags for sharks," Jack went.

"Does it say if anybody's been bitten at our beach?" my mom asked.

My father scanned the paper. "It doesn't say."

"Are there more waffles?" Jack asked. My mother gave him the last one.

"I'm not swimming with sharks," I said.

"I wouldn't let you swim with sharks," my dad said back. Then he grabbed my leg. I yelped. "Gotcha!" He laughed.

About an hour and a half later my parents were arguing in front of the lifeguard tower. Jack and I had dropped our chairs and bags. Jack's face was this combination of pissed off and bored both at the same time. He got that expression a lot lately, especially when we were around my parents. I was scanning the ocean for fins.

"Ridiculous," my mom was saying. "Other people are swimming, the lifeguards are keeping an eye—"

"I'm not trusting some nineteen-year-old with a shit pair of binoculars," my dad said. "You want the kids' feet bitten off?"

Jack had his earphones in and the volume turned way up. I tried to catch his eye, but he wasn't having it. He had barely talked to me in the car on the drive down. Just had his head buried in his laptop.

"Nobody else looks nervous or anything," I tried to point out, but my parents weren't listening.

"The kids can wade," my dad was saying. "It won't kill them."

"Excuse me," some lady said. She was talking to my father. He was blocking the board. Jack picked up his chair and bag and stomped away from us.

"There're sharks," my father informed her.

"Harvey!"

"Excuse me?" the lady said.

"Sir, we'd appreciate it if you'd move aside," one of the lifeguards yelled down. He had talked to my father forever already, explaining that the newspapers liked a good story and that the shark incidents south of us were too far away to be of much concern here.

"You're going to create a panic," my mother said. Not so quietly anymore.

"Don't you think you should at least post this?" my father called up to the lifeguard, waving the article around. It half fluttered into the face of the lady who was trying to read the board.

"Harvey, please," my mother said. Her mouth was getting tighter and thinner by the second. That *This is wrong, but there's nothing I can do* look. "I'm sorry," she told the lady.

It was embarrassing. I followed Jack and spread my towel out next to his. He was sitting up and scowling at the water.

"Everybody else is swimming." He'd taken his earphones out.

"Yeah," I said. "But what if we get attacked?"

"There's no sharks around here," Jack said. "Those other beaches where people got bit are sixty miles away at least. Dad's being so stupid."

"No swimming today," my father told us, kicking up sand, while he dumped the umbrella and his bag and chair.

"There's no sharks, Dad," Jack said.

"You're not swimming."

"Can we swim tomorrow?" I asked.

"We'll see," he said.

"Mom?" I went. "Can we swim tomorrow?"

She sighed and wiggled her toes in the sand. "I think you'll be able to swim tomorrow," she said.

"Why do you do that?" my father asked her. He had that tone. That edge. I glanced up at him. His face was red. The vein was dancing. My mother didn't answer him.

"Amanda," my dad said.

Jack got up and began to walk away.

"Where are you going?" I asked, but he acted like he didn't hear me.

"Why," my father was saying to my mother. "Do. You. Do that?"

I got up and ran after Jack. "We're taking a walk," I shouted back at my parents. My mother was standing, stiff, a half-folded chair dangling from her hand. My father was behind her, arms waving. You could hear his voice, picking and picking.

We walked all the way to the big fishing pier, which Jack said was close to a mile. It took us more than an hour, and we were hot. Tons of people were swimming, but we just dipped our feet. I splashed water on my shoulders and face. Jack didn't want his CD player to get wet, so he stayed at the edge, with the seagulls and sand crabs, staring out at the brown green horizon.

"I used to think it was under*toe,* as in *toe* on my foot," I told Jack when we were walking back.

He didn't say anything.

"Are you mad at me?" I asked him.

"No," he said, but it sort of sounded like he was mad.

When we plopped down on our towels, my mother was there alone, reading a book. I looked at the cover. It was called *Alive.*

"Where's Dad?" I asked.

"Walking," she said.

"I'm hot," Jack went.

"Don't make a fuss, please," my mom said. "I cannot take another fuss today."

"It's hot," Jack said again. "I'm going in."

"You may not go in. Dad said so explicitly."

"It's not fair," I complained.

My mother didn't answer.

"How come he gets to make all the rules?" Jack asked. "How come everything has to be his way?"

"Don't start," my mother warned. "This is the beginning of our vacation. Let's just have a good time."

"On a vacation," Jack told her, "you're supposed to be able to swim!"

I spotted my father walking toward us along the shoreline, his shaggy head bent down, looking for sea glass maybe. Three kids were jumping the waves in front of us, and not far from them two surfers were paddling. I didn't see fins anywhere.

Jack stood up. "I'm going in."

"Jack," my mother warned.

"Dad said you can't," I told him.

He'd gotten his CD player unhooked and his shirt off. He started walking toward the water.

"Jack," my mom said. "Come back."

"No," he told her over his shoulder. "It's so stupid."

Now my mother stood up. Her book fell onto the sand. Jack started jogging, and then he broke into a run and dived into the first wave, whipping out the other side. I looked toward my father's bent head. Then I looked at my mother, arriving at the edge of the shoreline, hand shading her eyes, calling to Jack. He stayed in the breakers, jumping, paddling, swimming. Mostly I just watched his back. When he leaped up, his slick shoulder blades looked as sharp as knives.

Even from a distance it didn't take my father long to notice. I could hear the shouting all the way from where I was, wiping sand off my mom's book.

"What the hell are you doing!" My dad broke into a run. A little girl in a lime green swim diaper sat back from her bucket and stared. A couple strolling arm in arm stopped.

Jack kept leaping. My dad raced toward him, stopping every few seconds to yell. "Get out of the water! Jack. Get out of the water!"

The three kids who were hopping the waves bodysurfed to shore. Jack kept jumping.

My father launched himself into the ocean, disappeared under a cresting wave, resurfaced right next to my brother, and grabbed Jack's arm. You could see him pulling and Jack shaking him off. Then you could see Jack change his mind and turn toward shore. My father kept grabbing some part of Jack. His shoulder, his arm. His hair. My mom stayed at the water's edge, her hands still shading her eyes. Jack clambered out of the ocean and right past her, my dad at his back, grabbing, while my brother kept snaking out of his hands.

"Don't you walk away from me," my father was shouting. Jack leaned down to grab his towel and shoes. His hair dripped on me. "God damn it!"

For some reason I looked over at the lifeguard tower. Weren't lifeguards supposed to keep things safe? They were just sitting there, staring along with everyone else. My mother seemed stuck at the shoreline, facing us. Her hand was still shading her face, like she'd forgotten it was there.

My dad kept yelling, "God damn it, Jack!" He was yelling so loud the little girl in the lime green swim diaper started to wail, and her mother scooped her up and started packing their cooler. He was yelling so loud that the arm-in-arm couple put their backs to the ocean to watch, as if my father were a geyser or a plane crash. Jack was trying hard to get away, up the dune and over its edge to the street, but my father wasn't letting him. He was stepping in front of Jack, so that my brother had to zig and then zag to make progress up the sandy incline. My father was screaming in Jack's face, and Jack kept moving, like a football player in slow motion. Step left, blocked, step right. Step right, blocked, step left.

Finally Jack faked right and then dodged left and ran hard up the hill, spraying a fan of sand behind him. My father shouted at his back, his voice filling the beach with ugliness.

By the time my dad stormed back to our spot, my mother and I had somehow gotten everything gathered together and were ready to go.

"What?" he snapped at my mom. She and I were filling our arms with chairs and blankets and bags. "What?" my dad snapped again, but my mother didn't answer him, and we trooped past the lifeguard tower and up the dune without anyone saying another word.

When we got back to the house, Jack was in his room with the door locked. My father threatened to break it open, and a few seconds later the knob clicked, and my father went inside. My mother hustled me out of the house, and we went to buy fresh shrimp, and she took a long, long time to decide which brand of cocktail sauce to buy. When we got home, my father was quietly reading the paper in the living room, facing the glass window.

I knocked on Jack's door, and he didn't let me in, but then I realized the door was cracked just the tiniest bit. I stepped inside. Jack was flat on his bed staring at the ceiling. His CD player and earphones were nowhere in sight, and his face was red and sweaty, eyelashes clumped wetly together.

"Get out," he said.

"Are you okay?"

"Get out!"

"Your door wasn't locked," I told him.

"I'm not allowed to lock it," he said. "Get out."

"But—"

"Get! Out!"

"I just want to help," I tried to explain.

He looked at me in a way I'd never seen before. With this expression that was brand-new. One that told me how small and disgusting he thought I was. "You?" he said, with that look. "You?" He snorted. "You're no help."

My mom is driving me to therapy. We tried to change the day because I wanted to be with Ellen when she got her new, short cast, but her doctor couldn't switch and neither could Frances, so that was that.

"Do you remember the summer of the sharks?" I ask my mom, tugging my hat down over my ears.

"That wasn't so long ago," she tells me.

"Dad didn't let us swim for practically the whole vacation," I say. I switch the heater vents to the floor. The air blowing from out of the dashboard bothers my eye.

"You and Jack got very good at paddle ball."

"Nobody else was staying out of the water."

"Well," she says.

"Why was Dad being so mean?"

"He wasn't being mean," my mom says. "He was being protective. Can we turn this down a little?" She's already turning the heat down a notch.

"Protective?" I go. "Try psychotic."

"Oh, Anna," my mother says. "What made you think of that?" She makes a right onto Bateson Avenue. We pass the mall. It reminds me I haven't been shopping in months. I need new shoes. And new underwear. I turn the heat back up.

"How come you let him do that to Jack?" I ask her.

"What?" she goes. "Do what?"

"Don't you remember?" I say. "Don't you remember him with Jack that first morning? Screaming and chasing him and everything?"

"Dad gets carried away," my mom says. "He gets scared easily, and then he gets carried away."

"Scared?" My father scared? No way. "He needs therapy," I say. "There's something seriously wrong with him."

"Did you hear that from Aunt Jerry?" my mom asks. I'm totally surprised.

"No," I say. "Why?"

My mom puts her thumb to her mouth and starts gnawing.

"You shouldn't bite your cuticles," I tell her. She drops her hand to the steering wheel. "Why?" I ask again. "Does Aunt Jerry think Dad needs therapy?"

"Can you get my checkbook out?" she says. I fish around in her purse and pull it out along with a pen. "You write it," my mom says. "I'll sign when we get there."

"You never do anything," I say, writing out Frances's name on the top line. "You never make him stop."

My mother glances at me and then back at the road. "I do the best I can," she says finally.

I fill in the date and the amount, and then I cap the pen and I think about it. What I'm trying to understand is, how can my mother say my father is scared, when really he's just a complete asshole? And how come my mother always stays out of things, reading her books or working in her study or floating out at the horizon, just letting him get away with it?

"I need to go shopping," I say. "I've got holes in my socks, and my boots are shot."

She pulls into the parking lot of Frances's building. "Okay," she says.

20

TODAY FRANCES IS WEARING PALE YELLOW PANTS THAT ARE SO
flowy they look like a skirt, and a matching blouse, scarf, and
vest. It's pretty. Ellen's mother has the same outfit, only she
doesn't wear it together all at the same time.

"I have SATs on Saturday, and then it's winter break," I tell
her. "Plus, Ellen's getting her short cast today. And my father
says I have to get better."

"Really?"

"He says I have to start driving soon."

"Nightmares?" She's pulling out her EMDR box and wires
from a black bag.

"Same," I tell her. "The dolphin and the wise woman help
me fall asleep. But then . . . you know."

"Heart attacks?" she asks. We both know they're not heart
attacks. They just feel like that in the moment.

"Not exactly," I say. "Just little ones sometimes between classes. I remembered to use the safe place once."

"Your Caribbean sea? The calm one with the turquoise water and the coconut smell?"

"Yeah. It worked when I remembered. But I didn't remember the other times."

"Do you have any idea what's triggering the anxiety?" Frances hands me the buzzers. *Triggering* means something that sets me off, gets me going into a panic.

"The idea of having to drive," I say, "a couple of times when I thought someone would ask me. But that wasn't at school."

"What about at school?" she asks. She helps me untangle the wires.

"I don't know. It's always in the halls, between classes."

We untangle, and she moves her chair forward a little and I pull up my legs, cross them, and put a suede pillow on my lap.

"All right," she says. "Are you ready?" She means am I ready to talk about the accident today. It's what we've been prepping for this whole time.

My heart starts speeding up. "My palms are sweating."

"That's fine," she says.

"No, it's not," I tell her.

"Anna, this isn't going to be comfortable."

"I know," I say. "You keep telling me that."

She puts the EMDR box down on the reddish wood end table beside her and looks at me. "I think you can do this," she goes. "You can ask me to stop or let go of the tappers anytime you want to stop. You have your safe place, if you need it, and you have your protector and your adviser. We told your mom

this might be a big session, and she's right outside in the waiting room, right?"

"Yeah," I say.

Frances's waiting room isn't as nice as in here. Just a few
hard chairs and a low coffee table with old magazines. I keep
meaning to tell her she should get some new subscriptions
or something, but then I forget, or I think it's rude.
My mother likes the pictures on the walls out there. One is
a framed poster of an egg. Just an egg. It is kind of nice.
Smooth and white and calm-looking. The other is a black-
and-white photograph of the sky with one cloud in it.

"Okay." I know I have to stop stalling. I wipe my palms on
the knees of my jeans. "Fine. I'm ready. What do I have to do?"

"I'm going to ask you some questions," Frances says. "I don't
want you to think too much about the answers. Okay?"

"Okay."

"At a certain point I'll turn this stuff on."

"Then what?" I ask.

"You just let come up whatever comes up. Images, memories,
thoughts, feelings, body sensations. Whatever. There's no right or
wrong. Sometimes you may notice something change and sometimes you may not. It can help to imagine that you're on a train,
and anything that does come up is just the scenery going by."

"Okay," I say. She's explained it to me before. I've heard
the train thing. I know that sometimes she'll turn the buzzers
off and ask me what's happening, and then I'll get to talk. I
know that I'm not supposed to censor anything or judge
what happens. I know all that. It's just hard to do what you're
supposed to do the first time you do something.

"So," Frances says. She picks up the EMDR box and leans forward a little in her chair. "Take yourself to the night of the accident." I nod and grip a buzzer in each hand. "Just remember."

"The tappers aren't on," I tell her.

"I know," she says. "That's okay. I'm not going to put them on until a little later."

"Oh," I go.

"Take yourself back to the accident and tell me what picture represents the worst part."

"The whole thing was bad," I say.

"Think of it as a mini movie," Frances suggests. "Watch it from beginning to end. Watch each frame."

"The thing I keep seeing," I say after a minute, "is my key chain dangling over me. It's just there, glowing in the dark, swinging, sort of."

"Okay," Frances says. "Now. What words go best with the image of your key chain that express your negative belief about yourself?"

"What?" I shift my crossed legs and lean harder on the pillow on top of them.

"As you see that picture, what is the negative belief about yourself?"

I have no idea what she means. She can tell.

"It would be a statement that starts with 'I am,'" Frances explains.

"I don't know." Everything was inside of me and outside of me in pieces and sideways and upside down and wrecked. "Maybe 'I am out of control'?"

"All right," Frances says. "And when you see that key chain, what would you prefer to believe about yourself now?"

"That I'm in control," I say.

"So how true do the words, 'I am in control' feel to you now on a scale of one to seven, where one feels completely false and seven feels completely true?"

Okay. For one thing, I'm getting a little sick of all these questions. And for another, I have no clue what she's asking.

"Can you repeat that?" I ask. So she does. The second time I think I understand. How true does "I am in control" feel now when I think about that key chain? Not very true at all, so I give Frances a two.

"What emotions do you feel now?" Frances asks.

Well. I feel the out of controllness and the wreckedness and everything sideways and upside down and in pieces, and it's awful.

"Scared," I tell Frances. "And guilty. Really scared and really guilty."

"On a scale of zero to ten, where zero is no disturbance and ten is the highest disturbance you can imagine," Frances says. Another scale? "How disturbing is it to you now?"

It's pretty bad. "A ten," I say.

"And where do you feel the disturbance in your body?" she asks.

"My heart is beating fast, and my hands are sweaty, and I'm all tense everywhere, and my face is hot." I'm thinking how she hasn't even turned on any buzzing and I'm already hating EMDR.

"Bring up the picture of the dangling, swinging key chain,

and the words 'I am out of control,' and feeling scared and guilty, and noticing your heart and hands and face and muscles, and go with that."

Go with that?

Then she turns on the box.

At first I'm just completely self-conscious. I mean, I'm sitting here with this buzzing back and forth in my palms, and Frances is staring at me, and the whole thing is so out there. Then the *buzz, buzz* in my hands turns into the *thrum, thrum* of Wayne's party that night, and it's not like I'm hypnotized or in a trance or anything. I know I'm cross-legged on Frances's red couch, but my mind speeds up too, and I can feel the *thrum, thrum* and taste the Jack Daniel's and see the signs not to party on the second floor and Seth's peppermint patties, and all these details I'd forgotten about.

"Just notice," I hear Frances tell me, and I realize I've closed my eyes. I keep them closed and keep noticing. It's like a movie on fast forward. Drinking and a pyramid of beer cans and someone wearing a bright pink jean jacket and Ellen walking me around the second floor, keeping everything under control. *Buzz, buzz. Thrum, thrum.*

"Take a breath," Frances says, and the buzzing stops, and I open my eyes and breathe in. "Let it go," Frances tells me, so I let the air out. She waits a second, and then she asks, "What's happening now?"

"I'm remembering the party," I say. "I got really drunk, and Ellen took care of me."

"Go with that," Frances says, and she turns on the box again.

There's Seth at the pool table, and then the green skin of the pool table turns into grass, and on the grass are small brown leaves, and my dad is screaming at me on the lawn, and then the lawn becomes the kitchen, and he's screaming at me in the kitchen, and behind him the laptop on the kitchen table shows the poker game, and the green of the poker table on the screen turns into our lawn, and our green lawn becomes the pool table in Wayne's basement, and I'm trying hard to sink the eight ball to impress Seth.

"Take a deep breath," Frances says, and the buzzing stops, and I breathe in and open my eyes, and she tells me to let it go and asks what's happening now.

"Different stuff," I tell her. Because I can't remember all of it. "I was angry at my father. We had a fight that night, and then I was playing pool. That was right before we left."

"Go with that."

I'm thinking how annoyed I'm going to get with "Go with that," but then I forget about it, and there's me and Ellen across from each other at the pool table, and Ellen saying something about how I'd rather be bitching about my father than be here, and then we're in the Honda, and I'm worrying she's going to throw up in the front seat and if she does, my dad will find out and be pissed off, and I'm going to pull over, even though she says I don't need to, and she leans down to do something to the radio.

. . .

"Deep breath," Frances reminds me, which is good, because it's weird how you can forget to breathe. "And let it go." She waits. "What's happening now?"

"I don't know," I say. My voice is all shaky, and I'm breathing heavy. "We've been hit." I huddle into the pillow in my lap and grip the buzzers.

My body's freaking out, and it's hard to catch my breath, and I'm having a heart attack, and there's sirens and Ellen's ponytail like glass in my eye and the smell of new plastic, and the earth dangling above, and "Hooow looong, hoow loong, how long . . . to sing this sooong?" and I feel Frances hand me a tissue box, but she keeps the buzzing going, and I open my eyes with it all happening so that I can wipe the tears with a tissue, and I just feel scared and ashamed and out of control, and I uncross my legs, knocking away the pillow, and I pull my knees up to my chin and keep hold of the tissues and wipe my eyes, and Frances goes, "Just notice, it's old stuff going by, just notice," so I try to keep noticing, and I get so tired, really, really tired, and then I'm waking up in the hospital bed, and my mother is there in her pajamas and raincoat, and she's telling me I'm okay, and then I'm in the car with my parents, and my father's saying, "She was in your lane, it wasn't your fault, she was in your lane," and then I'm in the hall at school, and Lisa is saying, "It was a cinder block," only I know it was a tree branch, and it was Cameron who swerved, not me, and then I see Cameron's silky hair and smoky skin, and I'm so sad I can hardly stand it.

Frances turns off the buzzing, and I take a huge breath and let it go, and I'm still half crying, and I try to explain, but it's hard.

"It wasn't me," I say. "I mean, I was driving, but it was Cameron out of control, not me. She lost control of her car. And it was out of control. I mean, the accident was an out-of-control thing, and I was out of control, but that's just because sometimes things can't be in your control, you know? And it's just really, really sad."

It's like colors and shapes of sadness and out-of-controlness, and I'm seeing them outside of me and feeling them inside of me, thinking how sad it is sometimes, things can be scary and sad, and I'm just watching it, and I open my eyes and let go of the buzzers.

"So many bad things can happen," I tell Frances. "There's nothing you can do about it sometimes. It's just the way things are."

She nods. "Go with that."

I'm thinking again how irritating it is that Frances keeps repeating practically the exact same thing to me, and then I have this memory of my father, enraged, saying, "Why are you repeating the same incorrect information?" And I get so mad, and I think about the words of the song in the car repeating over and over and over, "Hooow looong, hoow loong . . ." and I'm remembering when my father said, "Stop saying you're sorry," and I think, *I'm sorry, I'm sorry, I'm sorry,* and then that cop is going, "Okay. Okay. Okay. Okay," and then my body feels really heavy.

When Frances stops me and goes through her routine, I shrug. "I don't know," I say. "My bones feel like they weigh a lot, and I keep thinking about things with my father, and I'm sort of mad at him."

"When you think about the original incident," Frances says, "what comes up now?" I think of the image we started with. It's changed.

"The key chain is in the palm of my hand, and it's glowing really bright," I say.

She turns on the buzzers.

The key chain glows brighter and brighter, and it's warm and comforting, and the light of it shimmers, filling my hand with brilliant whiteness, and then the whiteness begins to expand and to hollow until it's a steering wheel made of milky white light, and I'm gripping it and driving, and Ellen's sitting next to me, her brown hair dancing in and out of the window.

"Wow," I go, before Frances can even say anything.

"Take a—" she goes, but I interrupt her.

"I know, I know." I take a deep breath and let it out, and I don't wait for "What's happening now?"

"I'm driving with Ellen and the steering wheel is this white light, and it feels okay."

Guess what Frances says?

We're driving in the sun, and it's this long, windy road, with the ocean along one side, sparkling and calm and clear, and even though I have this little knot in my stomach, mostly my body feels warm and relaxed, with the bright steering wheel solid and smooth in my hands.

I open my eyes. "You can turn it off," I tell Frances. She does. "I feel good," I say. "I really do. It's this pretty, curvy road, and I'm just driving with Ellen next to me, and it's totally fine."

"So on a scale of zero to ten, how disturbing is the image now?"

"A zero," I say.

Frances smiles. Her fang is sort of cute. "Do the words 'I am in control' still fit? Or is there another positive belief that fits better?"

"Do they fit with me in general?" I ask. "Or with the accident?"

"With the accident," Frances says.

"I guess. I think so."

"Think of the original incident and the words 'I am in control.' On a scale of one to seven, one being false and seven being true, how true do those words feel to you now?"

I think of the original picture. It's the earth key chain, only now it's dangling from the ignition while I'm driving on that windy road with Ellen and the sun and the ocean and everything feeling okay.

"Maybe it's not 'I'm in control.'" I change my mind. "Because something could happen out of my control."

Frances waits.

"Maybe it's more like 'I can be okay driving.'"

"All right," Frances says. "So I want you to pair your image with the words 'I can be okay driving.'"

She turns on the buzzers, and I go with it, and we're just driving and driving, and the earth key chain is swinging from the ignition, and it's all okay. Frances turns off the equipment.

"It still feels good," I tell her. "Still on that road. It's still sunny and pretty, and everything's okay."

"Close your eyes," Frances tells me. "Bring up the accident and the words 'I can be okay driving,' and mentally scan your body. From tip to toe. And just let me know if you feel anything."

So I do that, and mostly I feel calm, relaxed. "I feel fine," I tell her. "Except my stomach hurts a little bit."

"Go with that." She turns the buzzers on. Which surprises me because I thought we were done.

"My stomach hurts a little more," I tell her after a while. "But I still feel pretty good about the whole thing."

Frances glances at her digital clock on the windowsill and then has me imagine my safe place. I'm tired and time is almost up, so we don't do a lot more buzzing. Just enough to let me relax for a few minutes at that magical Caribbean sea with the dazzling turquoise water.

21

MY MOM DROPS ME OFF AT ELLEN'S.

"Where is she?" I ask Mrs. Gerson at their front door.

"In her room," Mrs. Gerson goes. She's smoking a cigarette.

"I thought you stopped," I say, stepping inside. Like, two years ago.

She cups her free hand around the back of my head. "I thought so too." Then she pulls me in a little, holding the cigarette out with her other hand so that smoke won't drift into my face. "See what you can do," she whispers. "She won't let me near."

I find Ellen in her downstairs bathroom, sitting on the lowered toilet seat. All she's wearing is her thick brown cable-knit sweater and her panties. Blue cotton bikini. She's holding a plastic razor in one hand and shaving cream in the other, and the tub is running, and she's crying.

It's bad. I didn't know it would be so bad. Her left leg from the knee down is skinnier than anything you've ever seen. It's about half the size of her right leg, and it's covered in dandruffy skin and dark, wiry hair. On the bony part of her shin a red spot, a sore about the size of a quarter, glares up from underneath the hair.

"I bet you didn't know pubic hair grew on legs," Ellen goes. It doesn't exactly look like pubic hair. But it's completely disgusting anyway.

"I thought you were supposed to get a shorter cast today," I say.

"They decided on that thing instead," Ellen says. "That thing" is a plastic and Velcro ski-boot-looking contraption lying on the back of the toilet. "Because it won't rub my leg as much as plaster, and I can take it off to bathe or whatever."

"Okay, look," I say. I lean down and take the razor and the shaving cream from her. I dip a washcloth under the running water and wipe it over her leg from the knee down. I get it as wet as I can without making a mess. Then I squirt shaving cream into her hand. "Start at your knee," I tell her, "and work your way down. Keep away from the sore." She obeys, still crying, while I fold a towel on the floor and then kneel on it. "Do you want to shave, or do you want me to?"

"I don't care."

"I'm afraid I'll cut you if I do it," I warn her.

"I don't care," she says again.

"Slide down to the edge," I tell her. She leans hard on my shoulder to maneuver her butt to the edge of the toilet seat. She winces, from her chest tube spot and from her ribs, and I wait until the wince is done. Then we stretch her leg over and across the tub until we can get her heel anchored on the built-in soap dish. I'm being as careful as possible because I have the definite feeling she's not even supposed to have "that thing" off for vanity reasons. Not that I blame her. "Here." I hand her the razor. She stops crying and starts shaving. One neat row, edged in dirty lines of hair-tinged shaving cream. Then another. After each one I pluck the razor from her fingers and hold it under the tub tap to clean it off.

"Your mom's smoking," I tell her.

"I know," she goes. "I smelled it."

I hand back the razor. "So. What did the doctor say?"

She starts another row. You can hear the hairs getting sliced off. That's how thick they are. *Snick, snick.* "The dicked-her?"

"Ellen!"

"I hate him," she says. "He didn't warn me about this. All he said—once—once, he said, 'Your leg will have lost a little muscle tone.'"

"How long do you wear the ski boot?" *Snick, snick.*

"He said six weeks," she tells me. Except for the round sore, ringed with a thatch of hair, her lower leg is fully shaved. The naked skin is pale and veined and scaly. "But now I don't believe anything he says. Maybe it'll be months. Years even."

She slowly scoots herself back onto the toilet seat. I reach for the Velcro and plastic thing.

"Not yet," she goes. "I took the dressing off." She means off the sore, I guess. "I wanted to see everything. I've got to redo it."

I bring her gauze and medical tape and Neosporin and let her deal with the shiny spot on her shin and then with the boot, while I mop up stray globs of shaving cream and rinse out the tub. When I'm done, I wipe everything down with the towel I was kneeling on. I throw the towel in the laundry hamper and let Ellen lean hard on me while she half walks, half hops to her room. She collapses on the bed, winces, holds really still for a second, and then breathes out slow.

"So guess what," I finally say.

"What?"

"I think I can drive now."

She gives me a glimmer of a smile. "Did you drive here?"

"No. I wanted you in the car with me the first time. If . . ." I stare at the plastic and Velcro. At how shriveled her leg is underneath. And I get scared a little. I can feel it in my stomach, flipping over. "If you'd be okay with that."

"Let's go to Top Hats," she says.

"Now?" I ask.

"You said you could drive," she tells me. "So, can you?"

"I swear," I tell her. "But my mom dropped me off here. I don't have the car."

"You can drive mine!" Ellen's mother yells from somewhere in the house.

"Were you listening to us this whole time?" Ellen shouts.

"Oh, for God's sake!" her mother shouts back.

There's this long, long silence.

"I can smell your disgusting cigarette!" Ellen finally calls.

"Do you want my keys or not?"

It's not a windy road with the ocean on one side and warm sun making everything shimmer, and there's no white light steering wheel. Instead it's freezing, and Ellen's not next to me.

She's in the backseat, and it took us ten minutes, with her mother helping, just to get her into the car. Ellen's not exactly happy, but I'm driving. I'm driving again, and I'm not feeling any sort of a heart attack coming on. Maybe I'm not in control of tree branches or cinder blocks, and maybe it's not totally okay, because Cameron's still dead and Ellen's lower leg looks like a broom handle, but it's okay enough. For now.

I wait a couple of days until I'm sure. Then I tell everyone.

Seth says, "Does your front seat go all the way back?"

Jason says, "Congratulations, Anna."

Lisa says, "You want to drive us to Patty's Saturday night?"

"Patty's?" I go. The last bell just rang.

Ellen left school an hour ago to get a short cast after all. It took only two days before the doctors figured out she wasn't keeping the ski boot on the way she'd been told to. They were satisfied that her sore seemed better and not infected, but apparently Ellen was unbelievably close to screwing up the break in her tibia all over again by wrenching it around in her sleep. Or trying to walk down the stairs on it in the middle of the night. Or something that pissed off her orthopedist enough he told her mother Ellen wasn't being responsible, and she had to go back to a cast. Something like maybe drinking and walking without the boot, I'm guessing. But for some reason I've kept my mouth shut.

Now the rest of us are at our lockers, filling our knapsacks.

"It's the SAT after party," Seth explains to me. "Patty's parents are going to be in Bermuda."

"Saint Bart's," Lisa corrects him.

"Oh," I say.

"But we don't have to go," Seth points out.

"Whatever." My throat is sort of closing up shop. It's not a fake heart attack. It's just . . . I don't know. It's something else.

"Really," Seth says. "We can hang out. Make out." He sees my face. "Count my send-a-dollar money or do origami."

"Origami?" Lisa asks.

"He's kidding," I tell her.

Jason says, "Forget the party." He swings his knapsack over one shoulder. "It's great that you're driving again." He arches his left eyebrow at Lisa, and she drops it. Then he looks at me. "Can I get a ride home?"

After I drop Seth off at his house, Jason switches from the back to the front seat.

"Ellen's getting a new cast," he goes. I turn right at the light and crank the heat. "You're driving again."

"Yeah," I say. The Honda still has that new-car smell. I like it, but Jack gets nauseous.

"So, I've got some news too," Jason goes.

"What?"

"I met someone."

"Really?" I make a left at Broad. "Where?"

"Taylor Academy."

"No way."

"Yes way."

"How did you meet someone at Taylor?"

"Online," Jason says.

"You're sure he's a kid and not some pervert?" I ask.

"Yeah." Jason nods. "I've already seen him a couple of times."

"What's his name?"

"Turn left at the stop sign. I can't tell you yet. He's not out."

"Oh," I say. I turn onto Bateson. "Ellen's going to be bummed." Whoops. I glance at him. "Um . . . ," I say.

Jason sighs. "It's okay, Anna," he goes. "I've known she likes me for a long time."

"She doesn't know you know, right?" I ask.

"I thought you two talked about everything," he says.

"What do you mean?"

"Take the left fork. She didn't tell you about our conversation?"

"What conversation?"

"Guess not. That's mine. The white one with gray shutters." I slow to a stop. "Ellen got drunk."

"When was this?" I put the car in park and keep it on. For the heat.

"A few weeks ago."

"A few weeks ago? Where was I?"

Jason shrugs.

"Where were you two?"

"My room," Jason says.

"Your room?" I ask. "Who else was there?"

"Nobody," Jason tells me.

"Where was I?" I go again. He shrugs again. Therapy? Was I at therapy?

"Anyway," Jason says. "She let me know then."

"She let you know?" I say. "Let you know? You mean, she told you?"

"Not exactly."

"Oh my God," I go. She made a pass at him. Ellen made a pass at Jason.

"Listen, Anna," Jason says. He turns his vents away from him and toward me. He doesn't know how that bothers my eye, so I punch the button on the dash to make the warm air hit our feet. "You know how much I like Ellen."

I nod.

"She's embarrassed enough as it is."

"She really likes you too," I say. "I mean, not just in a crush way. In a person way. She doesn't want you to be embarrassed either."

"Shit," Jason goes.

"What?"

A woman has opened his front door and is stepping out onto the front porch. She's wearing a long fur coat with a wool shawl wrapped around her head and black ski mittens on her hands. "Who's that?"

"My grandmother," Jason goes. "This is going to be bad."

"Does she live with you?"

"Yeah. I should go."

She's saying something to us. At least, I think she is. She keeps gesturing with her mittened hands.

"What's she yelling?" I ask him.

He looks mortified.

"You want to just get out and I'll go?" I ask. "I mean, I don't care if you have a weird grandmother. But . . . whatever you want."

He doesn't move. He looks at me. "Ellen really didn't tell you about this?"

"About what?"

Jason rolls down his window.

"Don't," I say. "It's too cold."

He keeps it down and then looks at me. Now I can hear his grandmother. She's craning her head at us in the car, and she's still waving her hands in the air, as if she's a preacher or something.

"'With a male as with a woman. It is an abomination.' Leviticus 18:22. 'If a man lies with a male as he lies with a woman, both of them have committed an abomination. They shall surely be put to death. Their blood shall be upon them.' Leviticus 20 . . .'"

Oh my God. I refocus on Jason, who's still looking right at me. He mouths the words exactly along with her shouting from their front porch.

"'Even as Sodom and Gomorrah, and the cities about them in like manner, giving themselves over . . .'"

"Oh my God." Did I say that out loud?

"Exactly," Jason goes. I guess I did.

"Ellen met her?"

"Well," Jason says. "She was sort of drunk." He tries a smile. "Ellen, that is."

He rolls up the window and his grandmother's voice fades, but she stays there, gesticulating on the porch with those mittens and that long coat.

"She lives with you?" I go.

Jason nods.

"She does that all the time?"

Jason nods again. "It's kind of entertaining," he says. He's not convincing.

"What about your parents?" I ask.

He shrugs. "They're not exactly thrilled either." I can't tell if he means about his grandmother or about him.

"That is the Bible she's quoting from, right?"

Jason nods. How can his parents let her do that to him?

"You were looking some of it up that night at Ellen's, weren't you?" My brain seems to be working, even though my heart is sort of stopped.

Jason nods again. "I stole it from the Gersons," Jason goes. "I could have just gone to the library or bought my own, but it was right there."

"Ellen knows," I tell him. "She doesn't care."

"It was stupid," Jason goes. "Cowardly. But . . . I guess . . ." He thinks for a second. "Cowards can be judged only from an unbiased point of view."

"I won't tell anybody," I say, not bothering to ask which back-seat book he's quoting from. "I promise. Seriously."

He stares out the window at his grandmother and then huffs tons of breath onto the glass, blurring her.

"Couldn't you even try being straight?" I can't help asking it. "I mean, not that I care. But . . . wouldn't it be easier?"

"I would love to be straight," Jason says to me. "Believe me."

I think about what it must be like to be gay. I let myself really think about it for the first time, without all the jokes and stupid assumptions. Jason pulls the door handle and lets in a blast of cold air and shouting.

"'Men with men committing what is shameful, and receiving in themselves the penalty . . .'"

"I believe you," I tell him.

Jack and I are eating pizza in the kitchen. Half spinach and mushroom for him, half cheese for me. My mom's at some faculty Christmas party, and my father's working late at the bank.

"I get the car this Saturday." Jack lifts a wedge from the box.

"Okay," I say. "I'll spray it with with that lemon stuff. It still has that smell you hate."

He looks at me funny.

"What?" I go.

"Nothing."

"Why are you looking at me like that?"

"Like what?"

"I don't know. Like that."

"I was just thinking about when we used to fight about the car."

"You mean when I was small?" I ask him. He tears at the crust with his teeth.

"Yeah," he says with his mouth full. "That's exactly what I mean." He's being sarcastic, though.

"You mean," I keep going, "like, less than six months ago?"

"Yeah," he goes. "I guess so."

We chew for a while and wipe our messy hands on paper napkins.

"What are you doing Saturday night?" I ask him.

"Rob's," Jack says. "We might go to Lucas's to hear this band. Frozen Shakespeare. Then maybe we'll go to Patty's."

"You're going to Patty's?" I put down my pizza slice.

"Maybe," Jack says.

"You're going to a party?" Somehow I thought neither of us would ever go to a party again.

"I was just thinking about it," he says. "That's all." It's the first time I've heard him sound guilty about anything. He sits back in his chair, leaving the pizza alone. "It's not like I'm planning on it."

I didn't mean to make him think I was accusing him of something. "You're allowed," I tell him. Because there aren't any rules. "You're allowed to go to a party."

We all signed up for the same location and day. I drive Lisa, Seth, and Ellen. Her new short cast goes from below the knee to the toes, and she uses crutches now. The wheelchair is gone for good.

Jason drives himself and meets us there. Only, he's a little late, and a few minutes after he rushes in, some other guy rushes in too, and they both look red in the cheeks. The guy has a blue sweatshirt on, with black stripes across the chest. TAYLOR ACADEMY is printed down the left arm. I glance at Ellen. She hasn't said a word about her conversation with Jason. I haven't told her about mine. It feels wrong somehow, but then again, so much has been wrong these past couple months that it doesn't feel as big of a deal as it could have, before.

The driving was fine. I can't wait to tell Frances. Only one blip from my chest for a split second and slightly sweaty palms. Other than that, a total breeze.

The testing is hard. At first I think my right eye is acting up again and making things blurry, but then I figure out what's really happening: The screen I have is greasy with fingerprints.

You'd think somebody would Windex them or something. It's a little distracting.

We get one break, during which we all gather in a huddle and share cupcakes. Seth brought them.

"Did you make these?" Lisa asks.

"My mother did," Seth says. "From scratch. Except for the frosting. She wanted to make that from scratch too, but I wouldn't let her. I like the kind from the can better." He licks some right off the top of his cupcake. "I bought a ton of it."

"With your send-a-dollar money?" Ellen asks him.

"Yep," he goes.

"How much have they sent so far?" Jason asks. He's glancing over at the sweatshirt guy. I see the sweatshirt guy glancing back.

"Seven hundred and twenty-one," Seth goes.

"That's a lot of frosting," I say. They look at me and crack up. I wasn't even trying to be funny.

But it's all ruined, after.

Kids are streaming out of testing rooms. It's a lot like the halls at school between classes. Only, everybody's more giddy. Like it's the last day of the year or the day before Christmas break. Stupid SATs.

"I'm driving with Jason," Ellen goes. She's leaning her back against the wall and her armpits on the crutches. Jason seems nervous. He's scanning the hall. This girl is shrieking and chasing some guy past us. She's pretty loud. I watch Jason keep scanning.

Then I get it. Oh my God. He didn't just meet Sweatshirt here. Jason *drove* Sweatshirt here.

"No," I say to Ellen. The guy being chased has buttonhooked back around, toward us again, and the girl is still running after him, screaming. She's screaming and screaming and screaming. "Drive with me," I tell Ellen.

"What's wrong?" Ellen asks.

"Nothing," I say. "Just go in my car."

"Is it the driving?" Lisa asks. "You're all red."

Seth nods and frowns. "You are."

I watch Jason catching Sweatshirt's eye. That girl won't stop screaming.

"I'm not red," I say. The running guy turns again, and the girl follows. Screaming and screaming and screaming.

Jason looks at me now. He seems really worried.

"Ellen's going with me," I say, to try and reassure him.

"You're sweating," Jason answers.

"What's going on?" Seth touches my face. The dark rings around the brown of his eyes are so beautiful.

"Are you okay?" Lisa and Ellen ask at the same time.

The girl chasing the guy is coming toward us again. Screaming and screaming and screaming.

"Would you shut up!" Ellen snaps as the girl passes.

And the screaming stops.

22

IF YOU HAVEN'T EVER KILLED ANYBODY, YOU MIGHT THINK THERE'S nothing worse than shaking and vomiting uncontrollably on the floor of the hall of the SAT building where about two hundred kids, half of whom you don't even know and one of whom is your sort-of boyfriend and one of whom is your best friend collapsed on the floor nearby in a mess of crutches, are staring in horror and have absolutely no idea what to do and will tell the story a thousand times tonight at the after party, without you there because you're home in bed stoned out of your mind on legal stuff, and then they'll tell it a million more times for the rest of your life.

Usually, Frances explains, we pick up where we left off the last time. It's Monday morning. I'm missing school. I'm an emergency. Usually, Frances reminds me, we work with an image. But today we're not going to do the usual. We're going to work with what's happening now. And what's happening now, she says, is not an image. It's the screaming. No, I tell her. It's not the screaming. It's the screaming, stopped. So that's what we start with: the screaming, stopped.

My negative belief about myself is "I am a killer." Frances won't let me use that one, though, because she says the truth is that I was behind the wheel when Cameron died, and even though I wasn't responsible for Cameron's death, EMDR won't change the fact that I was involved. So she asks, if I am a killer, what does that mean about me? I say I am very, very bad. She lets me use that.

Target: the screaming, stopped. Negative belief: "I am very, very bad." What would I rather believe? That I'm good, I guess. Right. On a scale of one to seven "I am good" gets a one. When I think of the screaming, stopped, what emotions do I feel? Terror, shame, helplessness. How disturbing are those feelings? A ten. Where do I feel it in my body? All over, shaking and heart pounding, and nausea and sweating.

"Go with that," Frances tells me. So I do.

23

IT'S DARK, AND SOMETHING IS POKING MY EYE, AND I'M CRUSHED on my left side, and Ellen and her blood are heavy, and the smell of plastic is underneath the screaming and screaming and screaming, and when the screaming stops, my body vomits, telling me that the screaming, stopped, is sickening, is somebody's life, stopped, and I want to wipe the heavy wetness off me and get up and run and make the somebody start screaming and keep screaming, to make them be alive, please, please, please, and it's like a wave of blood frozen in a massive curl, a big "Fuck you" to gravity and nature and everything that's supposed to be, and it's wrong, it should keep going, it should fall and roar over everything, but it doesn't, it's a frozen wave of screaming, stopped, of someone dead.

• • •

Frances is here, telling me to take a deep breath and let it go and what's happening now, and I see her certificates on the wall, with that left middle one all crooked, and I feel the cool, smooth suede of the pillow under my forearms and there's the red of the couch and the brown of her freckles, and I say, "It's weird how sick and sad I feel but also know that I'm here, and it's over."

And she says—big surprise—"Go with that."

And I'm thinking about how it's over, only it's not over. The screaming is over, and Cameron's life is over, and the beginning of my life is over, along with Jack's and Ellen's and Cameron's little brother's, and I see those two kids on the ocean trampoline, that brother and sister with those nut-colored eyes, and they're jumping, and then I see a little boy who looks just like Cameron, with natural platinum hair paired with dusky skin, and I think, *What's he going to do? What's he going to do without her?* And my brother's bedroom door slams, and I'm left on the other side, small and alone and not knowing what to do, and Frances is handing me her tissue box, and I feel it like waves, just waves of despair washing over me, and I cry and cry and cry, and my bones are soggy, and then I see Jack's head flat on the table, next to his laptop, and broken glass strewn across the living-room floor, and broken glass and flashlights glittering underneath the dangling earth, and the earth turns into soil, and then a blade of grass grows up out of the soil, and it's joined by other blades, and then there are brown leaves and fingers picking them up one by one, Jack's fingers picking up the leaves, and then his face looking at me, his face saying, *If you had just stayed home and picked up the leaves, maybe none of it would have happened,* and Frances turns off the buzzers.

There's all these balls of tissue in my lap, and I shake my head and cry, and Frances doesn't have to ask me to breathe or what's happening because I kind of get the rhythm of it all now, and so I breathe on my own.

"It's my fault," I tell Frances. "If I'd done what my dad told me to do, we'd have gotten to the party later and probably left later or earlier, and we wouldn't have been passing by Cameron on the road right at that second, and she could have swerved and been fine."

She doesn't say anything this time. She just nods and turns on the box.

The thing is, if you don't do what my father asks, he ends up being right, and you end up with serious consequences because you are just wrong and bad, and I see his face screaming and that vein and the spit at the corners of his mouth, and he's screaming and screaming and screaming, and I wish it would stop. I wish his screaming would stop, I wish he would stop. I wish he would die. And if you wish people to die, then you are very, very bad.

"Take a deep breath," Frances says. I breathe in, slow and long.

"I'm so mad," I tell her, and I'm crying again, and I tug another tissue, and she turns on her box, but I drop the buzzers and hold up my hand, and she waits, and when I can find my voice, I add, because it feels important, "And I'm scared of how mad I am. I mean . . . not scared exactly. Ashamed."

The word *shame* keeps marching by, like on a big city building's electronic ticker. *Shame, shame, shame,* just marching by, repeating itself in yellow bulbs over a black background, and it feels like I could throw up again, and my heart is heavy, and it moves across the screen of my mind: *shame, shame, shame.* And then my mother is there, curled around me, holding me tight with one arm and pulling a shade over the ticker with another, and I can feel her warm breath in my ear, and she's not far away in the corner of the house or fuzzy in the horizon, she's right here holding me and saying, "Shhh, shhh. I'm here, I'm here," and then I'm waking up in a twist of damp bedding from a nightmare, and my mother is still wrapped firmly around my back, and my father is there plumping my pillow, and Jack is there, watching from the doorway, and nobody's blaming me or thinking I'm bad, even though the sadness in the room is thick, like another blanket, twisted and heavy and everywhere.

I cry some more, with the buzzers off, and then I get this image with the sound gone, so there's no screaming, and no screaming, stopped.

"It's like a silent movie," I explain to Frances. "Everything is frozen. Ellen's ponytail and the cops, and Cameron lying on the pavement, dead. Even though I never saw her that night. I see her now. I'm sitting up, looking at her."

Guess what Frances says?

• • •

Cameron stands up out of herself, the way the movies show souls leaving bodies, and she walks over to me, and she kneels down, and she's all in one piece and perfect with those slender pink fingers and that skin and no blood, and she says, "You two are a lot more alike than you think," and she means Jack and me, and she floats away and up toward a lighted place far above us with a white sidewalk and wet green grass, and the echo of her voice says it again: "You two are a lot more alike than you think," and there's something comforting about what she's said because if it's true—and it must be, because dead people know the truth—then maybe I'm not so bad, because Jack isn't, because he thinks I can fly and tries to stop the waves.

"What's happening now?" Frances asks.
"I'm thinking about my brother," I tell her.

I see his shoulder blades, sharp as knives, slicing the water.

"I don't know," I tell Frances. "I'm tired. And if you say 'Go with that,' I think I'll scream."
She just looks at me and turns on the buzzers.

Screaming again, only now the screaming is different. It's not screaming like the way it was that night. The night of the accident. It's screaming like the way kids scream. Little kids. When they're playing. And then there's Cameron, a knobby-kneed girl, missing two front teeth. Her toddler brother is wearing nothing but a diaper, and they're playing in a sprinkler, which is going *snickety, snickety, snickety,* and young Cameron is squealing, the way little kids do when they're happy. And then I see me, and I'm my same age now, only I'm as small as a five-year-old, and I'm on the white sidewalk of this front yard where Cameron is skipping through the sprinkler, and I'm curled up in a ball, crying, and Cameron sees me and stops squealing, and she comes over, and she asks if I want to run through the sprinkler with her, and I ask if my brother can come too, and Jack is there, his age and size now, and he runs through the sprinkler and back, hogging it, and then he grins at us and says, "I can stop the water," and he presses his foot on the spout and the water stops and the *snickety* sound stops, and Cameron and I shriek at him, and her little baby brother stares at us with his droopy diaper, and then Jack lifts his foot and the water shoots out, drenching us all, and that's it.

"We're really little," I tell Frances. "We're playing outside in the summer, and we're all sort of shouting and squealing."

"And when you go back to what we started with, what do you get?"

I take a deep breath, and I try to get it back into my head. "It's hard to hear it," I say. "I mean, I know it happened, but I can't hear the screaming anymore. And I can't hear the stopped."

"What do you get instead?" Frances asks.

I try to think of that night. I try to think of the accident. Of that moment, when Cameron died, and I knew she died, even though I didn't know I knew it.

"It's not Ocean Road at night anymore," I say. "I mean, it is Ocean Road, far away in the background. But sort of in front of it and closer is this empty yard with wet grass and the sound of a sprinkler."

"How disturbing is it to you now?"

"It's still sad," I say. "And . . . I don't know . . . ominous a little bit." A good SAT word. How about that. "I don't know why, but I'm uneasy. But it's not as bad as when we started. So I guess it's at about a three."

"You've done a lot of work today," Frances says. She leans back a little in her black leather chair, and I glance at the clock. We're five minutes over. How weird. It seems like we only just started.

"I'm really tired," I say, surprised.

"Yeah," she nods. "That happens."

She doesn't make me leave right away, even though she probably has somebody else waiting. Instead she lets me close my eyes and imagine my safe place for a minute. We've ended like this before. I like it. The smell of coconut. The warmth of dazzling blue.

24

ELLEN'S BACK IN FLORIDA WITH HER PARENTS FOR THE FIRST
week of Christmas break. Lisa went to Cancún with her family,
and Rob's visiting cousins in Chicago. That leaves Seth, Jason,
and us. Usually my family goes skiing, but not this year. It's not
like we discuss it or anything. It's just that it doesn't happen.
Instead my father's taking only three days off at Christmas, and
my mom's doing a lot of shopping and grading.

Seth brings over a bunch of wrinkled envelopes and a family
pack of Hershey's Kisses. We count his send-a-dollar money
and eat the whole bag of chocolate and fool around a little. Well,
a lot. But somehow I start feeling nervous, and then I get bitchy.

Right as I'm kicking him out of my room, my father's walking up the stairs. He doesn't even wait until Seth's through the
front door before he starts.

"What was that boy doing in your room?" my father goes. I'm in the second-floor hallway, and my dad has one foot on the top stair and one foot on the carpeted landing.

"That's Seth," I say. He's a guy. Not a boy. "You've met him before."

"What was he doing in your room?"

"What do you mean?" I ask, even though I know exactly what he means.

"You know exactly what I mean," my dad goes.

I haven't had a nightmare for four nights, and I'm driving fine, and the shaking is gone. Plus, I haven't had any more panic attacks. Thank God. According to my father's initial orders, I have only one session left with Frances, but lately he hasn't mentioned anything about ending my therapy, so that's sort of in limbo.

I guess I thought maybe things wouldn't go back to as bad as they used to be, but now, with this old black knot in my brain, I figure I might be wrong. So I stand here, wondering what he wants me to say.

"Harvey?" my mother calls from their bedroom. She's wrapping presents, I think.

"What!"

"We weren't doing anything," I finally say, thinking about when Seth's hand slid up my shirt.

"Leave her alone!" my mom yells.

And then when that same hand slid down my pants.

"What were you doing in there?" my father asks me again, ignoring my mother.

Sometime between the shirt and the pants Seth placed a chocolate Kiss in my belly button with his mouth.

"We were just hanging out," I say. "Eating chocolate. And um . . . working on a project."

"You're not supposed to have food in your room," my dad says. "Bugs."

"We didn't make any crumbs."

"Or boys in your room."

"Since when?"

"Since now," he tells my mother, who's stepping into the hallway. She has a stray piece of Scotch tape stuck to her sleeve.

"I can't have a guy in my room now?" I ask.

"Harvey," my mom says. "Let's discuss this before we lay down any laws."

"There's nothing to discuss," my father says. "No boys in Anna's room."

"What about Jason?" I ask.

"Who the hell is Jason?" my dad goes. "And no."

"Jason's gay!" we all hear Jack yell from behind his closed door. A second later it opens. "Jason's probably safe, Dad," Jack points out.

My father still has one foot on the top stair and one on the carpet. "Don't get smart," my dad tells Jack. Then to me, "No boys in your room. Period."

"You let Cameron in Jack's room," I argue before I can stop myself.

My insides nose-dive with shame while my father's face goes purple. Jack's staring at the wood floor, smirking, of all things, instead of glaring with disgust at his despicable sister. While I'm trying to figure out how that's possible, my father is looking back and forth at Jack and then at me. "God damn it!" he says. He lifts his back leg and advances. His hand is raised.

"Stop it, Harvey!" My mom steps between us, and I dodge around both of them, down the stairs, to the kitchen, through the mudroom, to the garage, into the new Honda.

And then I just sit here. Because the last time something like this happened . . . well.

I turn the car on for the heat. I didn't grab a coat, and even though it's only three steps away, I'm not going back into the house for one. If I'd thought to bring my cell, I'd call Ellen, but I didn't, so I can't. I think about driving to Seth's, only I'm not up for facing him so soon after he's nibbled a Hershey's Kiss out of my navel. I could go to Jason's, only I don't even know if he's home, and what if he is and Sweatshirt is over there and they're in the middle of their own bag of candy? Or worse, what if he's home and Sweatshirt isn't there, but Grandma is? So I sit here with the engine idling, hating my father and hating myself more and shaking. And then I remember about planting my feet and breathing, and that helps a little.

About fifteen minutes go by. My brother walks out the mudroom door. He's holding my coat and wearing his, and he climbs into the passenger's seat.

"I'm sorry about bringing Cameron into it," I tell him right away. I wiggle my arms into the coat sleeves.

"It's because I'm a guy," Jack goes, completely ignoring the whole Cameron thing. Which makes me feel better. I can feel my gut relaxing a little bit.

"What do you mean, because you're a guy?"

"I'm not going to be getting pregnant."

"Oh, come on," I say. "Neither am I."

"He gets scared," Jack says.

"Where do you people get that from?" I ask.

"What 'you people'?"

"You and Mom," I say. "She says he's scared too."

"Well, he is," Jack tells me. "That's why he's such a mess all the time."

"A mess?" I go. "He's not a mess. He's a dick."

"He's that, too," Jack says. "But it's because he's such a mess."

"You always say I'm the one who's scared and a mess," I remind Jack. "If we're both so scared, how come he gets to be a dick and I don't?"

"That doesn't even make sense," Jack goes. "Do you really want to be a dick?"

"He was going to hit me," I say. "That's abuse. I could call the police on him."

"He didn't hit you," Jack points out. "Mom stopped him."

But I'm too mad at my father to let what my mother did sink in yet. "Are you defending him?"

"It's not about defending anyone," Jack goes. "It just is what it is."

"Since when did you get so Zen?" I ask.

"Since Cameron," he goes.

"You mean, since you knew her, or since she died?" I say it as respectfully as possible so he'll know I'm genuinely wondering and not just being sarcastic.

"Both."

His phone rings. You'd think, him being Jack and all, that he'd have it set on some awful song downloaded from the

Internet, but he doesn't. It's just a regular ring. He glances at the number, presses on the cell, and goes, "Hi, Ellen." Ellen? "Yeah. She's right here."

He passes the phone to me.

"I tried you first, so don't get all weird," Ellen says. "Did you know Jason has a boyfriend?" She sounds strange. Not tired exactly, but something.

"Um . . ."

"I just called him, and I heard someone in the background, and I thought it was you or Seth or something, but it wasn't."

"Maybe it was his mom," I say. Lame. How can I lie to Ellen?

"How can you lie to me?" Ellen goes. "I know you know something."

"I thought you just said you knew . . . ," I start.

"I wasn't sure," Ellen goes, and she starts to cry. "Now I am."

"It's a guy from Taylor." I'm a little surprised she's crying. It's not like Ellen to be this emotional over someone who was never even her boyfriend. "Jason just told me, and he didn't want you to feel bad, so he asked me not to . . ."

I hear Ellen kind of stop crying, and then I hear the slurp and swallow of her drinking. Drinking. Next to me Jack starts to get out of the car, but I grab his shoulder.

"Are you drunk?" I ask. Jack sits still.

"No," Ellen says after I hear her swallow. "I'm just having a couple of beers."

"Where are you?" I ask.

"In my hotel room," she says.

"You sound sort of drunk," I say. Jack looks at his watch. I look at the clock on the dash. It's 4:16.

"Don't tell Jason I even cared," Ellen goes.

"Were you drinking when you called him?"

"What's the difference, Anna?" Ellen goes. "My cell's dying. I have to find the charger."

"Wait," I say, but the phone's gone dead.

"She was drinking?" Jack asks.

"Do you think I should worry?"

"It's four in the afternoon," Jack says.

"Yeah."

"Huh." Jack's staring at me. "Your eye looks pretty cool. The pupil is vertical, you know. Sort of like a snake's eye."

"I prefer cat," I tell him.

The mudroom door opens again. It's my mom. She walks down the steps. I roll down my window, but instead of leaning in to say something, she gets into the backseat.

Jack and I look at each other.

"Um . . . ," I go. I've been reduced to *um* way too much lately.

"What are you doing?" Jack asks her.

"I have absolutely no idea," my mom says.

"Where's Dad?" I ask.

"Oh." She waves her hand, weary. "Ranting and raving somewhere on the second floor."

"He really needs some therapy," Jack mutters.

"Look who's talking," my mother says.

"What about you?" I ask her, and I sound mad. "You look who's talking."

"I am, Anna." She leans her head back on the fresh leather. And then she actually smiles at me.

"Oh," I go.

The mudroom door swings open a third time.

"What the hell are you all doing in there?" my father shouts.

We don't answer. He glares down at us. We look back. It feels like we're in one of those drive-through animal parks, and he's some strange monkey specimen. Usually the animals are in packs, though. Munching on something or rolling around or relaxed in a group squat, grooming one another. The thing is, my dad is just standing there. One person. All alone.

"Amanda?" he goes. "Jack?" He's squinting into the car at us, and for just a second I see something on his face. Worry or curiosity. "Anna?"

Maybe it's fear.

It was a striped-umbrella day, with slippery rafts and gentle undertow and the glinty sun reflecting off wet bathing suits. That morning there was a sandbar far out in the water, separated from the beach by green, lakelike ocean. So calm that my father said he'd swim Jack and me out there. Other parents were doing the same. Already the billowy swim trunks of fathers and the seal-slick backs of small kids decorated the water.

My father moved slowly between Jack and me, coaching Jack's seven-year-old crawl and my six-year-old breast stroke.

"Can I stand here, Dad?" I gurgled, halfway to the sandbar, arms and legs frogging madly.

"Not here," he said. "Too deep."

"Can you stand here, Dad?" Jack spluttered.

"Let me see." We stopped stroking and started treading while my dad went vertical and then sank straight down. I squealed, and my father's head popped up.

"Nope," he said. "Over my head here too. Swim."

So we kicked and paddled, the three of us side by side by side, until first my dad could stand on the sharp incline of sand, and then Jack and I could, and we were all on top of the bar.

"Neat," Jack said.

The water reached only to my knees, to my father's shins. It was like we were on an island. With our backs to shore, we could be smack in the middle of the sea.

"Look!" I pointed. Girls about my age had found a spot that seemed only top-of-the-feet deep. They were sitting on their behinds, making drip castles.

"Pretty unusual," another father said to mine.

"Anna," Jack went. "Let's find the edge."

"Never seen anything like this," my father answered. He caught a fugitive swim tube on his foot and held it there until a kid in a tie-dyed T-shirt and navy blue trunks plucked it off him.

Jack and I splashed farther toward the horizon, looking for the edge.

"It's there," some other kid said, pointing. She was older than we were. Ten or eleven maybe, and she was wearing a pretty yellow bikini.

"The edge?" Jack asked her. "Is that the edge?"

"I think," the girl said. She called over her shoulder. "Mom? Is that the edge?"

I looked where the girl was looking, to a woman who must have been her mother, standing not far from my dad. I saw the mother's mouth loosen and open, and then I saw my dad's eyes widen and his body straighten.

"Jack," he called. "Anna." His voice was sharp. "Come here."
Jack and I glanced at each other and then back at my father.
"Come here. Now." His face was pink. Was it the sun, or was
it him mad?

"Come on," Jack muttered.

We turned back. Then we heard a gasp. And another. The
father who had been talking to mine started running. It's hard
to run in shallow water. You have to sort of step high, and you
splash a lot. As he grabbed his son other parents began to step
high too.

"Matteo!" a woman yelled.

"Claire!"

"Lily! Catherine!"

My father grabbed my hand on one side and Jack's on the
other. He held on hard. It hurt. Why was he mad? What had I
done? My head began to fill with black fuzz.

"Now, listen." His voice was deep and like nothing I'd ever
heard. "There's a very, very big wave coming." Parents were
running and yelling and snatching up their kids. My father kept
us still. He was crushing my fingers. "It's going to break on us.
That means crash, Anna. It's going to crash on top of us. Hold
my wrist as tightly as you know how."

The steadiness of his voice helped the fuzz clear. My fingers
hurt, but he wasn't mad. I looked up and out. We were facing
the open ocean. And in the distance was a curl. It seemed small
to me. Long and low.

"Do not let go of me. Do. Not. Let. Go." My father's big
hand shifted to latch below my palm to my wrist. The way trapeze artists hold each other, flying through the air. I clutched

back. "Spread your feet apart and lean forward a little bit," my father said. I felt the sand suck at my ankles as I did what I was told. The curl was gliding closer and rising bigger.

Most of the other parents were clasping their kids to their chests and making for the shore. When I twisted to look, I could see frantic heads bobbing, arms reaching, legs kicking. "There may be more waves after this one that we can't see," my father said as it rushed toward us. His voice wasn't angry. It was patient. "I'm not going to let go of you." I heard more calls and screams and saw glimmers of color and flashes of bodies as parents lurched and kids scrambled. "You are not to let go of me. Hold on tight. Hold on. Hold on."

The wave was now directly in front of us, rearing and looming like some sort of sea monster with foam breath and a freezing roar. It was the biggest wave I'd ever seen. Bigger than five of my father stacked up. Louder than a thousand of him.

"Hold on!" my father shouted.

The weight of it blew my feet out from under me in an instant, the wet howling engulfed my head and body with weight, pressure. I held on as hard as I could. I held on and held on and held on, while the wave tried to rip us apart. My father gripped me so tightly that it felt as if my palm might tear off the stem of my wrist. So tightly that his hand and arm were shaking with the strain. Shaking and shaking and shaking against a wet force blasting down and around and through me.

And then the force was gone, and my father's shaking hand was yanking my wrist hard and high, and my body followed in a kind of jerk, sail, and drop, and I was on my feet, drenched and gasping for air, still gripping his wrist. I caught a glimpse of Jack, naked, and of my father's gray hair pasted sideways to his head as he spun us around, finally letting go of our hands, throwing us, hurling us in front of him, off the sandbar and into the water toward shore.

"Swim!" my father shouted.

There was yelling and a yellow bikini top floating quietly in my path. Adult bodies crashing through the water past me to the sounds of kids crying and lifeguard whistles.

"Keep swimming," I heard my father breathing from my left, my brother kicking hard on the other side of him. "Keep swimming."

My mother was at the shoreline, pushing aside another mother to get to us and with a towel to hide Jack's middle, and the edge of the ocean was filled with people hugging and scanning and crying and calling, while my mom hustled us to our spot, with our low-slung chairs and red-striped umbrella and sandy books, and Jack and I blew our noses into our towels, and so did my dad, and it made me and Jack giggle because it was gross to do that and we were never allowed, plus the commotion on the sand and in the water of all the people and lifeguards yelling and running, with the ocean so calm and peaceful now, seemed funny, like a sped-up cartoon, and then I stopped giggling, stopped short, because my father was huddled against my mother, and she was holding his big, wet head tightly against her neck with one hand and stroking his shuddering back with the other, crooning, "I know, I know," and I could see his entire body—legs, arms, back, bottom—shaking, shaking, shaking.

25

SETH AND JASON AND I GO TO THE MALL. IT'S THE DAY BEFORE
Christmas, and ridiculously, we all have a ton of presents to
buy. As we're walking past the insanely long Santa line I hear
someone calling my name.

"Anna!"

I look around. So do Seth and Jason.

"Anna." It's an Ashley. I don't think I've ever seen one without the other.

"Is she talking to me?" I whisper to Seth. He catches my
hand and slows down. So does Jason. So do I.

"Hi," I go to Ashley. She's standing next to this kid. He's not
little. He looks about twelve or thirteen. He's pudgy, with wide-
set eyes and a round mouth, and he's sort of drooling.

"How are you?" Ashley goes. She's wearing a down coat that

flares at the bottom and leather shoes with an amazing heel.

"Fine," I say, as if we actually know each other.

"How's Jack?"

"He's fine." Seth squeezes my hand. Little squeezes, one after the other, in a rhythm. Like a heartbeat.

"Hi, Jase," Ashley goes. "Thanks for sticking up for me in Gusty's class. What an asshole."

"Yeah," Jason says. "You're welcome."

Seth keeps squeezing.

"Listen—," Ashley goes, but then her brother interrupts her.

"Are you going to see Santa Claus?" He has a deep voice, sort of like Rob's.

"No interrupting," Ashley tells him. She puts her arm around his shoulders and looks back at me. "I've been wanting to tell you and Jack . . . and Ellen, too . . . that—"

"I'm going to see Santa Claus."

"Excuse me," Ashley reminds him. She sounds like a teacher. A nice teacher, but a teacher. Bizarre.

"Excuse me," he goes. "Now can I talk?"

Ashley sighs. "This is Matt," she tells me and Seth and Jason. Seth has stopped squeezing. His hand is still and warm in mine.

"Truck," Matt says. "My name is Truck."

We nod hello to him. The Santa line moves forward a little. We all move with it.

"Just . . ." Ashley wipes her perfectly polished index finger over Matt's drool. I could pass out from shock. "Ash and I have been saying for months how awful that whole thing was . . . and . . ."

"Ash!" It's Ashley Two. She's walking fast, dressed in cute boots with fur trim at the top edges and a pink-and-gray knit hat, completely model-like.

"Lee!" Matt yells, and he breaks away from Ashley One and nearly tackles Ashley Two.

"Truck!" She hugs him back.

My face is hot, and the place between my heart and my stomach feels all lit up. It's shame, I think. Because I'm sort of stunned to see them human, and really, that's so unfair.

"Hi," Ashley Two says to all of us. She throws Ashley One a look.

"I was in the middle of trying," Ashley One says.

Ashley Two turns to us. To me. "Mostly, we've been wanting to tell you and your brother and Ellen how much we . . ." She blushes. I've never seen an Ashley blush.

"We just felt so bad for you," Ashley One says.

Seth squeezes again. That's almost exactly what he said to me that day on the L of my couch.

"Thanks," I say. There's this awkward pause. "Nice to meet you, Truck," I tell Matt. Ashley One smiles at me. She has something that looks like a poppy seed stuck in her teeth.

"Nice to meet you, too," Matt says.

Jason and Seth and I are quiet for a long time after we leave the Ashleys. We walk by a bunch of stores on the second floor, spacing out from the quiet *sshuush* sound of the massive wall waterfall in front of the toy store. We end up at the courtyard with fake palm trees near the glass elevators.

"So that was weird," I finally say.

"I didn't know she had a retarded brother." Seth's trying to chew the head off a gummy bear.

"Down's syndrome," Jason goes.

"Ellen knew that," I tell them.

"Have you talked to her?" Jason asks.

"A few times. I need an earlobe massage." He moves around to the back of me and starts. It really does feel good. It probably looks weird, but it's incredibly relaxing. I have a flash of Cameron playing with her earlobe that day of the cake.

"Don't get too comfy there, tough guy," Seth tells Jason.

I take a deep breath. "Ellen doesn't sound very good."

"What do you mean?" Seth gives up on the head and pops the whole bear into his mouth.

"She's drunk a lot when we talk."

"Again?" Jason stops with my ears.

"Not drunk totally," I go. "Just . . . um . . . like she's been drinking."

"That sounds drunk to me," Seth says.

"Yeah."

"She seems pretty down a lot." Jason moves away. My whole neck is warm.

"I know," I say. "Her leg and ribs. And all."

"When does she get back?" Seth asks me.

"The twenty-eighth."

"There's your brother." Jason points. Jack's in the glass elevator with Rob, moving upward from the first floor. They've got a ton of bags.

"We just saw the Ashleys," I tell them when they step out.

Rob blushes and looks around.

"What are you getting Mom and Dad?" Jack asks.

I have no idea what to get them. "What are you?"

"I was thinking about a cat."

"A cat?" I say.

Jack nods. "Dogs are out, obviously, because of Dad."

"My father hates them," I tell everybody.

"Cats are pretty independent," Jason says. "You don't have to do a lot to take care of them."

"Mom's always wanted a cat," Jack says.

"Really?" I didn't know that. I make a mental note to ask her about it.

"I got my mother a gift certificate for a massage," Seth says.

"That's much better than a cat," I go.

Jack and I buy our mom a gift certificate for two massages. Jack finds four books on Texas Hold 'Em that we don't think my father owns.

Rob buys his mother a coffee mug with snowflakes all over it. He buys his father a mug with a bunch of cartoon bears. If you look really close, you can see the bears are in all these different sexual positions.

"What would your grandmother think of that?" I whisper to Jason. He raises his left eyebrow at me.

"You are so out there," Jack tells Rob, who just shrugs.

We end up in the food court, eating quesadillas.

"You know, you two look alike," Seth tells me and Jack.

"Shut up," we say.

Uncle Buck and Aunt Jerry come over Christmas Day. They leave their dogs at home. They give me a silver pendant with an opal stone. They give Jack a year's subscription to this Web site where you can mail-order DVDs for half price. They give my parents plane tickets and hotel reservations to go to Paris for a long weekend in the summer.

"We can't accept this," my mother goes.

"You have to," Aunt Jerry says. "They're nonrefundable."

"It's too much," Mom argues.

My father stays quiet. I know what he's thinking. He doesn't want to miss a Friday and Monday of work.

I give Jack these new headphones that shut out the sound of ambient noise. He seems to like them. He gives me a professionally framed photo. The colors are bright and clear: yellows and whites and blues and grays. It's of the ocean. Specifically, of a wave. Huge. Sparkling.

"How did you know?" I ask him, gaping.

Jack looks pleased but confused. "What do you mean?"

I stare, astonished.

Jack shrugs. "I just saw it in that gallery at the mall," he says. "I thought you'd like it."

Later, as I'm standing in the doorway of my room examining my walls to figure out where to hang it, I overhear my mom and Aunt Jerry walking up the stairs.

"I started last week," my mom is saying.

"Do you like him?" Aunt Jerry asks.

"We'll see," my mom says.

Normally I'd mind my own business.

"Started what?" I call. I step back out of my room and into the hall. My mom and Jerry are at the landing. "Like who?"

Jerry looks at my mom. My mother sighs and looks at me.

Normally she wouldn't really answer. "My new therapist," she says.

"Does Dad know?" I ask.

"Of course," Mom says.

"Oh."

Seth has to spend all of Christmas Day with his family.

"I only have a minute," he tells me at the edge of our lawn, by the street, next to his car.

"I know," I say. We're bundled up in hats and scarves and down and Gore-Tex.

"Merry Christmas." He hands me a long white box. "Don't open it out here," he says. "It's too cold."

"Is it roses?" I ask. My father is allergic to roses. Seth kisses the tip of my nose and then my mouth. His lips are freezing. So is his mint breath. "See you," he goes.

Inside I open the box, and my mom helps me find a vase and trim the stem bottoms underwater, on an angle.

"Oh my God." I'm reading the card.

"What?" my mother asks.

"I'm getting a dozen roses on the first of each month for the next year," I tell her.

"That's a lot of money," my mom says. "Where is Seth going to get all that money?"

"In the mail," I say. She frowns. "It's a long story."

"It would have to be." She sounds like Ellen's mom a little when she says that. I kind of like her sounding that way.

"All I got him was a stupid gift basket." With dozens of candy packages surrounding bubble bath, food coloring, and a sweater. Lame, lame, lame.

My mother hands me the vase. The roses smell sweet, and they're this deep red and a little over the top. "You never told me he was your boyfriend," she says. She glances at me and pulls a bottle of baby aspirin off the shelf next to the sink. She shakes out two pills and drops them into the vase. "It would be nice if you told me things every now and then." Her voice sounds careful.

Suddenly I wonder about how popular she is with her students. All those excellent evaluations. Does she hang out with them on campus? Do they tell her things? I wonder what she thinks about when she's in her office, up there on the third floor. Or reading her survival books.

"What?" she goes.

"Nothing," I say. "What about Dad's allergies?"

"We'll see if they kick in," my mom suggests. But then she doesn't have any other ideas.

"What are the aspirin for?"

"They make flowers last longer."

The carefulness of her voice, and the way she stepped between my father and me the other day, make me feel sort of formal for some reason. "Thank you."

"What if we break up before the year is over?" I ask Seth over the phone.

"Oh," he says. "Does that mean we're going out now?"

"Funny," I say.

"Don't worry so much, Anna," he goes.

"But that's what I do," I tell him.

"I know. But if we break up, I'll just change the address with the florist and have them sent to my mother."

"Seth!" I go.

"Okay. To your mother."

"Seth!"

"Come on," he goes. "Do you even like my present a little?"

"A lot," I say. Why can't I be nicer? "But that's so much money. Ellen wouldn't approve." I'm not telling him about my dad's allergies. I don't have the heart.

"Ask her," Seth says.

I hang up with him and dial Ellen. It's their last day in Florida. It's still early, and I'm hoping I won't hear the sound of beer in her voice. I don't, so I tell her about the roses.

"I think it's the most romantic present I ever heard of," Ellen says. "And it's a total waste of money, and you'll never get treated this well by anyone again, so you might as well enjoy it."

I hang up on Ellen and dial Seth.

"See?" he goes. "Told you so."

On top of the lemons and perfume, now Ellen's house smells like pine needles. Her mother puts their tree up the day after Thanksgiving each year and takes it down the day after they get back from wherever they've vacationed.

Ellen's moving a lot more smoothly with her crutches now. Her cast looks sort of beaten up, though. It's dingy and the edges are grayish. She's written stuff all over it. Not sentences. Just words. *Panacea. Absinthe. Mired. Avuncular. Thrice.*

"I think you should have a certain New Year's resolution," I tell her. We're back in her old room. She can do stairs. She's not nimble on them or anything. But she can do them.

"Like what?" she asks. She's hanging up a bunch of new clothes onto wooden hangers. I'm pulling them all out of shopping bags, cutting off tags, and handing items to her.

"Like no more drinking in the daytime."

She bangs a hanger onto her closet bar and then turns to frown at me. She has this way she can lean one armpit on a crutch and sort of balance like that.

"What's that supposed to mean?"

"That I think you have something weird going with alcohol."

"Oh, please." Ellen rolls her eyes. I try to hand her a pair of brown wool pants with cuffs at the bottom, but she won't take them from me.

"You can be mad," I say, and I feel strangely calm. "But that's still what I think."

"Right," Ellen snorts. "Because drinking and all that intimidates you. You're just scared of everything."

It's not only that I'm tired of hearing that. I mean, I consider it. I really do. But this time I know she's wrong. I can feel it. "A little scared," I admit. "About different things. But not the way I was before." Something about my voice or my face gets her attention. She drops her sneer and flops down on her bed. Then she winces, but her face doesn't grit itself the way it used to. Her chest tube sore is basically healed, and her ribs aren't far behind.

"You seem so different lately," she finally says.

"I am," I say. "We all are." She knows I mean her and me and Jack. "It's bad," I tell her. "Drinking a bunch of beers alone in the afternoon is bad." She massages her neck. "You don't have to be a rocket scientist to know that much."

"It's not a bunch of beers," she tries. "And you're no rocket scientist."

"Obviously."

"Wow," she says. "One meeting with the Ashleys, and you can be a better bitch than me."

"See?" I go. "You just called them the Ashleys."

Ellen rolls her eyes. "Okay," she says. "I won't drink in the afternoon."

"You better not," I tell her. "I mean it."

"I know."

Christina Noonan throws a New Year's party. We all go, which is different to begin with. Because, among other reasons, I've never once been to the same party as my brother. And the last party I made it to was Wayne's.

Ellen gets a little drunk, but I can't yell at her because it's New Year's and not in the afternoon.

"He'll be here," she keeps telling Jason every second. His boyfriend was supposed to show up. She's trying to be supportive.

"When we want something, we always have to reckon with probabilities," Jason goes.

"Absolutely." Ellen takes another swig from her beer and then gets up to go pee for the eightieth time.

Jason plays with his right earlobe, and Seth pulls my curls and feeds me chocolate-covered pretzels between sips of beer. The truth is, I hate the taste of beer.

Right before midnight Ashley One and these two guys and these three other girls grab me.

"It's your brother," they say. "Come on."

They lead me and everyone to Christina's parents' bedroom, which has an OFF-LIMITS—NO JOKE—STAY OUT OF THIS ROOM sign on it.

Jack's inside sitting on the edge of a canopy bed. His arms are crossed over his gut, and his head is slumped over his arms, and he's bawling.

"He's really drunk," Ashley One tells me. "Carl's been trying to get him to throw up."

"He never vomits," I say, the ink everywhere, heavy and ugly.

"Never?" somebody asks me.

"Not in his whole life," I say. Black and thick.

We hear people screaming outside the room. "Ten! Nine!"

"It's the countdown," I tell everyone.

"I'm finding Rob," Ellen goes, and she leaves the room.

Jack is trying to suck in air between sobs. Seth and Jason stand by the door, their feet wedged against the bottom, making sure nobody else walks in.

"Jack." I sit next to him, sinking with weight.

"Six! Five!"

Jack's body is heaving. He's moaning. My teeth start to chatter.

"Great party," somebody mutters.

"Get the fuck out of here," I hear Jason snarl, while Ashley's going, "You asshole!" and there's movement and the door is opening and closing, and I don't even know who's in this room anymore.

"Jack," I go. I ball my hands into fists to keep them from trembling.

He tries to say something to me, but he's crying so hard I can't understand him.

"What?" I ask. "What?"

"Want it . . . stop."

"What?" I say again. Sinking. Sinking.

"Make," Jack gasps. "Time . . . stop." Drowning. "Make . . . it stop."

"Two! One!"

"I can't," I say, helpless. Seth is here, next to me, leaning down toward us, swallowing and swallowing.

"Make it stop," Jack begs me.

"I can't."

Seth and Jason and Rob haul Jack into Rob's car. Rob's sober, thank you, God. He drives me and my brother home. We try to sneak Jack upstairs, but my parents are in the kitchen, just back from their own party, and they catch us.

"We're drunk," Jack tells them. And then he passes out.

26

MY FATHER DOESN'T TALK TO ANY OF US ALL THE NEXT DAY. HE can't really talk to Jack because my brother keeps his door locked. My dad doesn't even try to force him to open up.

I arrange myself on the L of the couch and watch TV and whisper on the phone to Ellen and to Seth.

My mother stays in her study in the corner of the third floor.

My father sits in the kitchen playing poker, swearing and humming, and getting up to pace the house every hour or so. I keep hearing him stand up, walk the stairs, creak around the third floor, then the second, then back down the steps, through the entryway and family room and living room, past me, and back to the kitchen.

"Dad," I say on his fifth tour.

He stops walking.

"Tuesday's my last therapy session, if we're still going by what you said when I started." He stays quiet, which, truthfully, makes me nervous. "But I want to keep seeing Frances." He touches his fingertips to his chin.

"Dad?"

"All right," he says. And he goes back to the kitchen.

Frances's freckled face looks windburned. I wonder if she went skiing over the holidays, but I don't ask.

"Everybody's had a pretty challenging time," she says after I'm done telling her what's been going on. It's such a therapist thing to say. Then she asks, "Do you have any ideas why you have so many mixed feelings about going out with Seth?"

I shake my head a little and feel tired. I wonder why, of all the things I've told her, that's the one she decides to ask me about. "It just seems hard." I don't even really know what I mean. "It's another person you have to . . ."

"You have to what?" Frances goes.

"You have to . . . I don't know. Take care of. Not piss off. Not disappoint."

"That's what a boyfriend is?" Frances asks.

"I guess that's not how other people see it," I go, feeling stupid.

"You like Seth, right?" Frances asks.

"A lot," I admit. "He's really funny and nice and sort of weird, but in a cool way."

"You like the fooling around?" Frances asks.

"Frances!"

"Well?" She smiles. A wide smile. That fang. "Fooling around is a big part of romantic relationships."

"Yes," I tell her. "I like it."

"You enjoy how you feel when you're with him?"

I nod.

"But not enough to want to take responsibility for his happiness?"

"I guess," I say.

"What if you were to consider the possibility that in relationships you're not responsible for the other person's happiness?"

"Huh?"

"That maybe we're responsible for our own," Frances says. "Other people can help or hinder, or sometimes both. But in the end it's up to each of us."

"It's hard for me to see it that way," I tell her. "I mean, if you mess up with someone, they can't handle it and they don't like you, and you feel awful and it's just not worth it."

"Is that right?" Frances asks.

"Plus, people leave."

"Leave?"

"You know. Break up with you or break your heart or . . ."

"Or?"

"I don't know. They just leave you. They . . . they . . ."

"Die?"

"Why are you being so mean?"

"I'm not trying to be mean," Frances says. "I just had a feeling that's what you were thinking, and so I said it for you."

"Well, what if I didn't want you to say it for me? What if that's not even what I was thinking?"

"Then, I made a mistake," Frances says. "And I'm sorry."

I stew on that for a while and stroke my suede pillow. Then

I say out loud what's in my head. "Why should I get to be happy with somebody as amazing as Seth when Jack will never be happy with someone again?"

She waits awhile, but I don't say anything else, and she doesn't speak for me this time.

"I think that question is one we should definitely talk about," she finally says. I don't say something back about it. I can't go there right now. That whole topic just makes me tired.

"Aren't we supposed to do EMDR today?"

"Nice dodge," Frances goes. She looks at me without moving for just long enough to let me know she's not going to forget to bring it up again. "But yes." She pulls out the gray box and starts to untangle the wires. "Let's start by checking what we did last session."

"It's hard to remember," I say, getting myself situated with legs up and crossed under my pillow.

"That's okay." Frances hands me the buzzers. "Just tell me, when you do think of the work we did last time, what comes up?"

There was the key chain. I can see it dangling from the steering wheel made of light on that bright day by the windy road. Also there was the thing about screaming. But what I remember more is wet grass.

"Sprinklers," I tell Frances. "Wet grass and little kids playing in the sprinklers."

Frances nods and turns on the buzzers.

The sprinklers make that *snickety, snickety* sound over and over, and all that black, wiry hair on Ellen's leg, with the razor going *snick, snick* over and over, repeating and repeating, and then the black hairs turn into green blades of grass strewn with brown leaves the size of barrettes, and I'm picking them up and saying, "In order to add fractions, you have to find a common numerator," and my father is standing over me, glaring and vein-popping, screaming, "Why are you always repeating the same wrong thing?" And there's dread and weight and blackness, and he's looming, like a monster, screaming and screaming, and I try to pick up the leaves, but they crumble or blow away under his monster breath, and it's my fault because I'm repeating the same wrong thing over and over, always wrong, always bad, and it's better to be still and calm, but I can't do it, it's never right, I'm bad, always so bad.

"Take a deep breath," Frances tells me as she turns off the buzzers. "And let it go." It's wild how you forget to breathe sometimes.

"It's my father," I tell her. "He's mad. He's yelling at me. I hate the way he always yells and makes up his stupid rules at the drop of a hat and won't let you even say anything."

"Go," Frances says.

My father's face bloats and then lengthens and gels into a brackish green wave, and my brother has his feet planted and his arms up and out, and he's going, "I can stop the wave, Anna! I can stop the wave!" Only, he can't, and the father face breaks hard on top of us, and Jack yells for me to help, only I'm no help, I'm no help at all, I can't help Jack, and Jack can't help me because it's too much, too fast, and another one rears above us, and the vein in the temple ripples and froth foams at the mouth, and it crashes, and there's nothing you can do because it's so much bigger and smarter and stronger than you and it knows what you deserve anyway.

"I have a sour taste in my mouth," I tell Frances, and she keeps the buzzers going. "Like I'm going to throw up, only I'm not, and it's this feeling of desperation and despair and dread, and I hate it. I so hate it."

"Just notice," Frances tells me in her steady voice.

Another father face looming and rearing and screaming and crashing black noise over and through us, and another and another and another, and our feet are planted wide and our heads are ducked low, bracing ourselves for wave after wave after wave after wave.

"I hate him," I tell Frances, clutching the buzzers. "I hate him. I hate how he can't stop. He never stops. He never stops and you can't breathe or move, there's never any room, and I can't stand it, I can't stand it."

He's crashing down on us, down on me and Jack, and we struggle to stay standing, to breathe, we struggle under that wave and then another and another, and then suddenly there's a pocket of air and we suck it in, gasping, just as another father face lifts and poises to strike, and Jack is clutching my hand, and the wave above is roaring, howling, only somehow it isn't angry anymore, it's afraid, it's a wave afraid to hurt us and afraid of us getting hurt, and the mouth in the wave is a circle of fear and the eyes are wide, and it's straining not to crash, shuddering and shaking with the effort because the gravity of the tides and of the moon and of everything is stronger than anything, and when it can't stop itself anymore, the father face cascades down on us, screaming, "Hold on! Hold on!" And Jack and I wind our arms together, clasping each other's wrists, like trapeze artists, gripping so hard we're shaking and trembling, but we still hold on, we hold on, even though we can't stop the waves, even though we can't stop anything, we hold on together, and it helps.

Frances turns off the buzzers and hands me a tissue. I see those stupid certificates and some fresh tulips in a vase, and inside I notice that I'm wondering where she got tulips from in the middle of the winter and if she put aspirin in them, but what I say is, "I don't know." Frances waits, and I blow my nose. "I just see me and Jack and my father, and it's just . . . I don't know. Emotional."

Jack and I are underneath rushing and blackness and weight and pressure, but we're holding on to each other, side by side, feet planted, heads down, hands gripping wrists, and we hold on and hold on and hold on, and it helps, it helps a lot, and then the wave has passed, and there's no more, there's really no more, and we squint out at the horizon to make sure, but the ocean has morphed into a magical Caribbean sea of dazzling turquoise, and we're standing next to each other in the warm, soft water. Calm and still and peaceful, with a barely moving ship on the horizon and a V of pelicans gliding above. We look behind us, and on the pink sand, by the red-striped umbrella and damp towels and low-slung chairs, my parents are lazing in the sun. The brim of my father's white hat is tilted low over his eyes, and the strap of my mother's straw one is tied firmly under her chin. We're looking over our shoulders, back at them, and they see us and wave, and in my father's hand is number 1,000 coconut sunblock, and Jack and I turn back to the ocean, side by side, palms cupping the surface of the beautiful, beautiful blue water.

"Look," Jack says. "Minnows."

27

"HERE," I SAY, SHOVING MY SIXTH BOUQUET AT JASON. WE'RE IN Ellen's room, upstairs. It's June, and I've had to give all my roses away because as it turns out, my dad started sneezing and swelling immediately with the first one.

"Thanks," Jason goes. But he doesn't take them from me. His eyes are puffy.

"I'm really sorry," I tell him. Sweatshirt cheated on him. With a girl.

Ellen takes the flowers and leaves the room, probably to find a vase. She barely has a limp anymore. At first when she got the short cast off, she walked sort of funny. Tippy-toed. She couldn't get her heel flat on the ground. But now she's moving pretty smoothly.

Jason flops onto Ellen's bed. He's half sitting on Whitey, but

I don't say anything. He leans back and stares at the upside-down dried roses hanging from Ellen's ceiling fixture. I gave her bouquet number four. My mother got number three for her office, and Seth got number two, just for kicks.

"He was so mad about prom. I should have taken him." Jason took Ellen to prom instead of Sweatshirt. As friends, obviously. None of us thought our school could handle two guys going together. Not yet, anyway. Maybe in a couple of years.

"For someone who wasn't even out until he met you, that seems totally unfair," I tell Jason.

The prom committee thing turned out to be not so bad. I ended up tagging along with Ellen and Jack to most of the meetings anyway, and nobody cared that I was an unofficial member. Jack wanted to DJ prom himself, but he got voted down because even though he's pretty popular, nobody much likes his music, and we hired a band instead. But Jack did manage to convince the band and the committee to let him set up movie clips on a big screen on one side of the gym, and everybody thought that was completely cool.

Seth and I spent so much time fooling around outside on the football field that a bunch of people said they thought we hadn't shown up at all. Lisa started liking Jack and wanted to go to prom with him, but he hasn't liked anyone since Cameron, and especially not Lisa. So she went with some guy she met at the mall who Ellen and Jason reported was cute, but who didn't say a word the whole time.

"Besides which," Ellen goes, walking back into the room with a vase full of water, "what's he fooling around with a girl for if he's gay?" She sits at her desk and starts arranging the roses. "He's confused, Jase."

Jason starts to cry again. Well, not cry exactly. It's more of a weep. Which makes me think about Seth. Which makes me think about sex. Which makes me internally slap myself so that I can focus on Jason, who needs his friends.

"You deserve better," I tell Jason. "A lot better than that guy."

"Yeah," Ellen says. "You need someone like Keith."

She's sort of dating some guy she met in physical therapy who smashed his arm in another car wreck. He looks a little bit like Bono, but he's not all that charismatic. I like him, though, and he likes Ellen, and that's good enough for me. She still drinks too much at parties, but she's stopped drinking during the day, and Keith is on my side about the whole thing, so that's good.

"If Seth cheated on me, I think I'd die," I tell Jason. He's stopped weeping.

"Especially if he cheated on you with a guy," he points out.

"Don't," I go. "Do you think he's gay?" Panicked, I'm remembering all those rumors about Jason and Seth after the accident.

Ellen snorts. "No way."

"You'd never fool around with him, would you?" I ask Jason. "That would be, like, insanely cruel."

Now Jason snorts. "No offense, Anna," he goes. "But no way."

"So have you guys done it yet?" Ellen asks. She's finished with the roses. She spins around on her desk stool to look at me. She means have we gone all the way, made it home, gotten busy, done the dirty. Had sex.

But she knows we haven't. She's just trying to distract Jason.

"Stop trying to distract me," Jason goes.

"Fine," Ellen goes. "You're sitting on Whitey." Jason lifts his butt, and Ellen gets off her stool to pull Whitey free. She starts rubbing him over her chin. "I know you know I made a pass at Jason," Ellen goes to me out of the blue. Then she blushes.

"You told her?" I ask Jason.

"No." Jason arches his left eyebrow and looks at Ellen. "How do you know?"

"Whitey told me."

"How would Whitey know?" I go.

Ellen shrugs. "Whitey knows everything."

When I get home, my parents are in the kitchen. The weird thing is, it's my mom yelling instead of my dad.

"Responsibility!" my mom's saying. My father's sitting at the table in front of a Texas Hold 'Em online game.

"What's happening?" I ask Jack, who's in the family room on the L-shaped couch with his DVD paused. Somehow I get the feeling this fight has been going on for a while.

"Mom's pissed," Jack says.

"Mom's pissed?" I can't remember the last time my mother was the one who was pissed.

"Bullshit," my father's saying, only kind of weak.

"You can't tell anything from two sessions!" my mom yells. "It takes time, Harvey. It takes time and effort!"

"The guy's an idiot," my dad says back. "I'm not going to sit in some room with an idiot for an hour a week and pay him for idiocy."

"This is not a debate," my mom goes. "This is an ultimatum!"

"Damn it," my father says. "I had three aces."

We hear a crash and then silence.

Jack and I look at each other and then race to the kitchen doorway. My father's laptop is on the floor. Someone knocked it off the table. He and my mother are staring at it.

"You can't really force someone into therapy," Jack says into the quiet room. He should know.

"This is none of your business," my mom answers.

"Bullshit," Jack goes.

"Yeah," I say. I feel strangely calm. "Bullshit."

"Go to your rooms," my father tells us, still staring at his laptop.

"You can't make someone go to therapy," I say. "But you can be really pissed at someone for a long time for not going." I look hard at Jack when I say that.

"I said," my dad repeats, "go to your rooms."

We ignore him. We go back to the L-shaped couch instead. Jack unpauses his DVD. It's footage of some god-awful band.

"What's this one called?" I ask him after about three seconds.

"Mystic Circles of the Young Girls. It's good, right?"

"Yeah," I say. "Right."

I hear him crying through the wall in the middle of the night. I kick off my sheet and pull on decent pajama bottoms and the TALK TO MY AGENT T-shirt and leave my room to go to his. In the hallway I stop short, surprised to see my mother, her ear an inch away from Jack's closed door. She straightens up in her slippers and looks sheepish for a minute. We watch each other listening to Jack for a while, and then my mom motions for me to follow her. She leads me to the kitchen and makes us peanut butter and jelly sandwiches.

"Are you taking Jack and me to Paris if dad won't go?" I ask her.

"We'll see," she says.

"Do you think Jack's going to pick NYU or UCLA?"

She chews her sandwich for a while without answering.

"Mom?" I say.

"NYU," she tells me. "Please pass the milk."

Jack won't do therapy.

"It really helps," I try to tell him one Sunday afternoon after Seth has left.

"Leave me alone, Anna," he goes.

"With EMDR, your brain makes these little movies in your head," I tell him for the tenth time. "I mean, some people's do. Mine does. Yours probably would. You'd like that."

"I know," he says. "You've told me about it ten times."

"Even Dad's in therapy," I argue.

"Twice. To some guy he thinks is a moron," Jack says. "That's not exactly therapy. And you don't see him going back, do you? Besides, it's not a competition."

"Ellen says it's totally ironic that out of the whole family you're the only one not even willing to give it a try."

"Ellen is too smart for her own good," Jack goes.

"I heard you crying a few nights ago," I tell him.

"Shut up."

"I just want to help," I say.

He throws his pillow at me. "Yeah," he goes. "I know."

I still haven't looked at the memorial Web site for Cameron. Frances and I talk some about it and do some EMDR, and it's not bad the way it used to be, but I don't want to click the final click. I don't want to read what everybody has to say about Cameron and how she's not here. The screaming, stopped, doesn't haunt me the way it used to. It doesn't haunt me at all, actually, but the sadness isn't something you can buzz away. It's just sad, and even though I know it's not my fault, it's still sad.

So it's not like you live happily ever after. It doesn't work that way. You still have bad dreams sometimes, only instead of waking up drenched and shouting, it's more like you wake up really tired in the morning, feeling that sadness and thinking, *That was so awful. That was such an awful thing that happened.* It's not like my mother doesn't still spend tons of time up in her study and my dad doesn't yell at all of us for little things. It's just more that none of it feels as terrifying and out of control. As lonely.

Mostly you realize you can handle it. You'd rather turn it all upside down and dump it out and watch it scatter and disappear. You'd rather do that, because you don't want to have to handle it. You really don't. It's too stupid and crazy and incredibly, incredibly unfair.

But you do handle it. Because the thing you learn is that you can.

ACKNOWLEDGMENTS

The author gratefully acknowledges and warmly thanks:

Dr. Bennett S. Burns, Dr. Steven Covici, Dr. Mark Klion, and Dr. Kevin J. Mickey for their speedy and thorough courses in ophthalmology and orthopedics;

Gina Colelli for accepting endless requests for information and assistance, and for her sensitive supervision of EMDR;

Ann Griffin for making AP biology a surprising pleasure;

Richard Jackson for encouraging without pushing, and then patiently waiting;

Stephen Lucas for his love, support, and band names;

Dr. Tanya Lucas for her medical expertise and for connecting me with Dr. Covici and Dr. Burns;

Amy Rosenblum for suggesting that Grandma be calmed down and Dad be kept on the beach;

Dr. William Rosenblum for catching blood-alcohol level inaccuracies;

Charlotte Sheedy for so readily supporting the path I requested; and

Mike and Anna Stewart for connecting me with Dr. Klion.